# Tales From a Mortician

## Twenty Twisted Stories of Horror

### By
### Michael Gore

Enter the Gore!

AuthorMike Ink

www.AuthorMikeInk.com

First Published by *AuthorMike Ink*, 10/13/2012

www.AuthorMikeInk.com

*AuthorMike Ink* and its logo are trademarked by *AuthorMike Ink Publishing*.

Printed in the United States of America

*For Nicole,*
*You are more beautiful in death,*
*Than you ever were in life.*

# Table of Contents

# INTRODUCTION
BY
MICHAEL ALOISI

Michael Gore, as a person, is more interesting than most stories you will ever read. In fact, I'd love to write a book about him one day, though I doubt he would ever let me. How I met Michael is also very interesting....

My friend's father died and though I didn't know the man myself, I figured I should support my friend and go to the wake. As uncomfortable as it was for me to look at the dead body of a stranger, I did it, sat down for ten minutes and quickly snuck out the door. It wasn't until two hours later did I realize I had lost my cell phone. Realizing I left it on the chair next to me in the funeral home (I was rudely, but inconspicuously sending text messages while sitting there), I raced back to get it before they left the building for the night. When I arrived, most of the place was in the dark, but the door was still unlocked. Walking into a dark, empty funeral home at night is a story in itself. I almost wet myself. Trying to be quiet, I snuck into the viewing room (trying not to look at the body) and found my phone on the floor under a seat a few away from where I was. As I got up to leave, I noticed a portly man had come in and was talking to the corpse. I didn't recognize him and was about to ignore the man when I saw him go inside of the corpse's jacket. I stood silently until the man left, he hadn't noticed me.

Being a writer and insanely curious, I had to know what the man stuffed inside of the jacket. I had done similar things with dead relatives, leaving them a memento or a note, but I was sure this man did not know the deceased. Holding my breath and doing my best to not look at the dead man's face, I lightly pinched his jacket, pulled it open and with one quick snag, I had the papers. Getting as far away from the body as I could, I went to the back of the room and opened them up. There, on white lined paper, written in sloppy red ink, was the story *Home Liposuction,* which is in this book. I sat reading it, enthralled with the story. It was clever, gross and interesting. Why on earth had this man put it in the dead guy's suit coat?

It took a bit of snooping around the place, but I was able to find the man in the embalming room of the funeral home. Walking in, the stench overwhelmed me, and the sight of a dead body on a table with the blood being drawn out of it almost made me faint. I was in so much shock I couldn't speak, Michael rushed me out of the room and sat me down in some sort of break area. After a glass of water, I was able to talk. At first the man denied that he wrote the story and put it in the jacket, but after some prodding, he put his head down like a scorned child and admitted to the act. When I told him I loved the story, he gave me a quick glance and a small smile graced his face. Asking why he put a story in the man's pocket, he again looked down. I had to ask three more times before I got answer.

"I never thought anyone would like my stories, so I, I bury them with the dead. I really don't know why, but the idea of my stories, stuck for eternity underground with a body… comforts me." I did not question or even try to figure out how that made sense to him, but I did ask if he had any others stories that I could read. He was reluctant at first, but when I told him I was a writer and really loved his stuff, he agreed. I was then handed the story, *Blood Soup*, again, I loved it. He joked about how this story was his vision of himself if he was a woman, I couldn't help but laugh.

Michael and I talked for several hours that night, mostly about horror movies and different novels and stories he loved. He even showed me his collection of *Fangoria* magazines. He had every issue in very nice bags, stored in numerical order. This man took his horror seriously. With a lot of effort and much coercing, I asked him if he would let me read his work from now on, rather than him putting them in coffins, or if he still felt the need to do so, that he made copies for me first. Begrudgingly, he agreed.

Over the course of the next several months I would visit him from time to time to read his work and talk about horror. It was an enjoyable friendship, even if we only met in the break room of a funeral home. It took almost a year of our friendship before I got him to agree to let me release his work to the world. Michael is painfully shy and wants nothing to do with the living. The story, *Dead Love*, is practically a female version of himself, though he ensures me he has never inappropriately touched a body.

After much talking, an agreement was made with several conditions set in place. One, his real name would never be released as he didn't want to lose his job. It was he who came up with the pen name Michael Gore. He wanted to use Michael as a thank you to myself, which I found flattering, and Gore as a nod to the horror industry. The second condition was that he never had to do any publicity, interviews or have anything to do with the outside world. There have been successful, reclusive writers before, so I agreed. He also requested that I be the one to go out and publicize his book for him. Being that I already travel to promote my books and work closely with the horror industry, I agreed. Lastly, he asked that when the book is released, that we fill a coffin full of copies and that we bury it in the woods, just him and I. The thought of wasting so many copies made me cringe, but I agreed and a deal was made. By the time you read this, the blisters on my hands from digging a hole in the woods should already be healed.

Now, almost two years after I first met this man, I am proud to have this book in your hands, rather than rotting underground with some corpse. I think Michael's stories are gripping, gross and worth reading. In this book you will experience terror, be disgusted and enjoy a roller coaster ride of twenty short stories filled with death, revenge, serial killers, ghosts and the beyond. If you love horror, I am sure you will love these tales… and if you do, you'll be happy to know that Mr. Gore has a lot more stories and even a few novels he is eager to have me read. In other words, there might be a lot of Gore in your future.

-AuthorMike

# DON'T LET THE BED BUGS BITE

*If you feel an itch under your skin, it's too late.* The doctor was quoted saying.

Jane pushed the laptop away, feeling a shiver run down her spine. The article was creepy, terrifying actually. It wasn't some story or movie she watched, it was *real* and it was *happening.* For weeks she had been watching the news reports; watching the epidemic spread from a few hotels in New York City, to state after state… now it's the biggest outbreak since the Black Plague. *Bed bugs…* who thought they would be more than a gross nuisance? Almost everyone has heard the saying at one point in their life before going to bed… *Don't let the bed bugs bite.* Jane's mom used to say to her as she kissed her on the forehead and tucked her in each night. Now it wasn't a saying… it was a warning.

Sipping her coffee she closed the lid of her laptop, not wanting to think about the bugs anymore. The idea of those suckers getting in her house made her want to take a shower. It was all *anyone* talked about, she just didn't want to think about them anymore. Flicking on the kitchen television she realized she wasn't going to escape the news of the bugs. Every channel had constant coverage of the epidemic. They used charts, graphs and fancy touch screen monitors to show the outbreaks. They used menacing voices to tell viewers that it will keep spreading, that the worst was yet to come and that they still haven't found a suitable pesticide to get rid of the bugs. She tried to click past the news reports, but they were to mesmerizing. It was like a car wreck, you couldn't *not* look at. Besides, she probably should start to prepare for it, the outbreaks were getting closer.

Pouring another cup of coffee she stared at the television screen, unable to look away at the death toll numbers. It was in the hundreds of thousands, it was worse than any disease in history. The scary part was the deaths only started two months ago. At first it was just a horrible outbreak of rashes and bites on people. All they had to do was change their sheets and disinfect the house, but it got worse as the bugs adapted. They said it was a new type of bed bug, a new breed they had never seen. Instead of just biting you, these bastards got under your skin… literally. They crawled in your ears, nose, eyes and…other orifices while you slept, some cases even found that they bit their way through your skin to get inside your body. The scientists were saying that they were not feeding on us, they were just using us for the warmth and moisture… using your body like a dog house. You wouldn't know they were in your system; that they were burrowing through your insides, laying eggs and making homes out of your bodies until it was too late. As the news article said, *if you felt an itch, it was too late*, there was nothing you could do. They asked that if you had that tickling sensation or saw the bugs in your bed that you should spray paint an X on your front door, leave and get to one of the thousands of emergency medical stations set up across the country. Of course they didn't tell you that all they would do was burn your body once you died from the bugs burrowing into your heart, lungs or other vital organs.

The worst part was there was no cure, no surefire prevention. You could spray around your house, but the sprays were not that effective. They didn't kill them; they merely repelled them, a bit. Most businesses and all stores were shut down. Only electric plants and water facilities were being forced to stay open. Unfortunately for Jane her husband, Jay, worked at the power plant. That is what made the situation so much worse for Jane, for leaving the house left them open to bringing the damn bugs home.

When the epidemic started they were smart enough to stock up on enough canned and frozen food to last them four months, more than what the government recommended. According to the experts the less physical contact with the outside you had the less chance you had of picking up the bugs; especially since they clung to porous material like clothing. Wearing anything but a rain coat was like wearing a magnet for them. Touch or get too close to any material, couches, chairs, curtains, car seats or even tissues and the bugs would be able to jump from that item and attach to your clothing. Even one single bug on your clothing could cause your house to be filled with thousands within a week, if it was a female that is. And since they are dominant, the chances were good. This was a huge financial burden for Jane and Jay. To keep from contaminating their house Jay had bought one hundred pairs of t-shirts and shorts that were all factory sealed in plastic bags. They kept the bags in the garage and everyday Jay would leave the house naked, get dressed outside and go to work on an old dirt bike they bought off a kid down the street. The bike was another caution, no porous material on it and the wind helped blow bugs off if they attached (at least they hoped). Every day after work he would ride home, get undressed in the farthest corner of the backyard and burn the clothing in an old trashcan. After that Jane would spray him off with the garden hose, the worst part of Jay's day as the water never got above fifty degrees, before he came in the house.

A picture of the microscopic bug flashed on the screen. It was simply terrifying. With the naked eye it looked like a tiny black or brownish dot. Yet with a microscope, it looked like something from another planet; a tick from Hell; a horror movie reject. With its sharp pinchers (which they explained were used to cut their way through your insides), pointed back hind quarters (which made extraction nearly impossible without tearing a chunk of flesh out), jagged shell and evil little face and tentacles, Jane couldn't understand how anyone could look at the picture without itching all over. As she was doing now. It was horrible because at times you felt phantom itches all over your body; you scratched yourself raw and wondered if you had them in you. Jane started to cry; a regular occurrence these days. She just couldn't help but wonder how many people would die, if she would die, if her friends and family would die, before this was all over, if it would ever be over. There were enough people preaching that it was the end of the world. Whole cults killing themselves before "Satan" could get in them. It was a nightmare.

Jay had been telling her for days to ignore the news. That she should watch nothing but DVD's or movies On Demand since eighty percent of the remaining channels did nothing but cover the bugs. She would argue that she didn't want to pretend they didn't exist, but at the same time he would come back with the fact that watching non-stop coverage was doing nothing to help and everything to hurt her emotionally. With a deep breath she found the strength to turn the television off. In the silence she thought about shaving her head and pubic hair off, like some of the doctors had suggested. It was drastic, but it seemed to be the new line in prevention. People were wearing plastic or leather clothing so the bugs couldn't attach to them, then they found out they could attach to any body hair. A study showed that a third of the population had shaved off all their hair, every last strand of it. Maybe she'd wait for Jay, maybe he could do it to her, he shaved himself anyway. It would be fun, maybe they would laugh for the first time in ages.

The day went by like usual, unbearably slow and boring. She didn't feel like watching another movie and she couldn't focus enough to read a book so most of the day was filled with pacing. Especially since she avoided sitting on the couch, love-seat and bed; they were porous. At first they started to get rid of anything that they could stick to, but they quickly realized they would have almost nothing left in the house. Even though she knew the bugs would get her if they were in the house, regardless of where she sat, she still felt uncomfortable on the couch and bed.

Staring out the window she didn't realize how much she missed the yard or even just outdoors. It had been weeks since she left the house. The closest she got to the outdoors was when she stood in the garage doorway and sprayed Jay down. The fresh air in those moments was always wonderful. She tried to remember how nice the yard used to look, its green grass, red mulch and flowers, it was paradise. Now the grass was hip high, turning brown like wheat. The flowers were dried up and gone, weeds grew out of everywhere. There was a deep desire inside of her to go and mow and plant and prune, but as she saw a fly zip by the window she was reminded of the millions of unseen bugs that were out there. Turning the cold handle to shut the blinds and the outside world out she saw something she hadn't seen in a while, a person.

Jane pulled the blind wide open, squinted hard and saw that it was her neighbor, Ashley…and she was covered in blood. Instinct kicked in. She ran for the front door, pulled back the dozen locks, opened it, opened the screen and froze when she saw the sheet of plastic in front of her face. She was suddenly sucked back to the reality that she shouldn't go out there. Ashley might be infected, and if she was, the bugs could jump onto her, get into…. As she started to step back she saw a hazy figure through the plastic, it grew quickly and suddenly hit the sheet in front of her spraying red across it. Jane stood frozen as she watched the hand streak a trail of red behind it as it ran down the flimsy barrier.

"J, j…Jane, please…" there was a horrible coughing noise followed by another huge splat of red, this one much deeper in hue.

"I, I need help, I'm cut, please, dear God, please Jane." The plastic was starting to push in towards her, just a few more pounds of pressure and she'd break through and contaminate her house. With the sole of her shoe Jane kicked as fast and hard as she could at the hand. She heard a sickening snapping sound followed by a howl. Suddenly her neighbor's whole body was pushing against the plastic, she was screaming and pleading. Finding the courage Jane backed up, shut the doors and locked them. After a few seconds she heard the plastic rip, the door rattle and then all the noise fell silent. Ashley had either given up or died, either way she was happy the assault was over.

Leaning over she squinted one eye and looked out the tiny hole. All she could see was a blur of red. Just as she started to lean back there was an intense smashing sound behind her, instantly she knew it was a window being broken open. Opening the front hall closet she grabbed the loaded shotgun that Jay taught her how to use and went to the window she had been looking out moments before. Sure enough it was smashed. One of her decorative yard rocks lay on the carpet on top of a pile of glass shards. Readying the gun she slowly stepped forward, glass crunching under foot. When she was three feet from the window one mangled hand flew over the sill followed by the other. The sight stopped Jane in her tracks. Both arms were cut up, bleeding and filthy. They gripped the ledge and pulled up to reveal the face of what was once a beautiful woman. Jane had to stifle vomit at the sight of Ashley. Half of her dark hair had been ripped out in chunks. An ear was missing, her nose split open down the middle; there was a hole in her right cheek and one eye looked to have been gouged out.

"Get...it...out...of me!" Ashley gurgled. Jane wanted to push her back before she pulled the trigger, but she didn't want to touch her, didn't want to contaminate herself. Stepping back, she planned on running upstairs and locking herself in the bedroom, but she was trembling so hard... the gun went off. Ashley's head exploded like a watermelon sending chunks and blood everywhere, including on Jane....

The reaction was instant. There was no hesitation, no shock. Jane threw the gun aside, spit out the glob of iron tasting goo from her mouth and immediately stripped her clothing off. Naked she raced up the stairs and into the bathroom. The sanctioned, "safe room" that they removed all porous material from and sealed off the room just in case of an instance like this. Racing inside she turned the shower on full blast and dove under the icy water. The cold slapping her face and chest released the scream she had been holding in. Grabbing the hard brush they left hanging around the shower-head she scrubbed her body furiously as the water warmed up. Over and over again she pushed the hard bristles into her skin scraping and scrubbing off the spots were the blood had hit her. Her skin instantly became red and raw. It became painful, but she couldn't stop herself from scrubbing, that is until she thought about her hair.

The chunks of Ashley had gotten on her hair, if one of those little bastards were in the globs they could have attached to her. Grabbing a bottle of bleach from under the sink she jumped back into the shower, held her breath and poured it over her head. As the bleach ran over the countless fresh scratches on her body she felt a pain like nothing she had ever experienced. Dropping the bottle she fell to her knees, vomited from the over powering smell and crawled out of the tub. Her hair fell in front of her eyes. What was once a beautiful brown was now blotched with white spots and a kaleidoscope of different shades. She had to get rid of it.

Jane stumbled her way through the house, dripping wet and in pain. Finally in the garage she dug through three drawers before she found the electric razor Jay used to cut his hair off with every three days. Plugging it in she went to work shaving herself. Her groin first, the thought of those monsters eating their way into her through there was unbearable. Her pubic hair came off rather quickly; her head on the other hand was a different story. Being wet the razor clogged and protested every few inches. Finally fed up Jane bent over, letting her hair hang down and cut big chunks off with garden sheers, then resumed using the razor. It took a while, but she got it all off.

Running her fingers over her head was a sensation she never felt before. Her mind was so scared and flustered, she didn't know how to feel about it. As she stood there with a pile of hair at her feet she started to get cold and realized how exposed she was. She had to get back to the bathroom. Sprinting full speed up the stairs she realized that the shotgun was a necessity, in case anyone else tried to get in. With slow steady breaths she walked back down the stairs and into the living room. She did her best to keep her eyes on the floor, to avoid looking at the woman she used to have coffee with every Saturday, without a head, a head that *she* shot off.

The gun was half under the couch. Ten feet of carpet covered with land-mines of skull, brain and teeth lay ahead of her. She did her best to hop around all the chunks, but it wasn't good enough. On her tippy toes her left foot landed on a large glob, red and pink meat squished through her toes. Jane paused for a second, glanced at the gun and realized it too was covered and decided to just go for it. Running flatfooted, shards of skull poked the soles of her feet while strands of hair and blood stuck to her toes as she grabbed the gun. She did her best to shake off the chunks and ran up the stairs again, trying to wipe each foot on the carpet with each step.

Back in the sealed bathroom she once again turned the shower on. The water was warmer this time as she washed off her stained red feet. The gun was in the shower as well; she did the best she could to keep it from getting completely wet. When the water started to run cold she realized she was as clean as she was going to get. Shutting off the tap she sat down in the tub, hugged her knees and cried as she waited for herself to air dry.

With her body and tears dried up she was ready to think about her situation rationally. It was too late for their house, it was now contaminated. She was probably safe in the bathroom, as long as she didn't already get infected. The major problem was she had no phone, food or way of telling time. It still had to be early. She could easily make it without food until Jay got home, but she would need a way to somehow warn him before he came into the house. Even if she did warn him and he got to her without getting infected, what would they do then? They couldn't stay in the bathroom forever. They'd have to flee, but where? Friends and relatives wouldn't risk taking people who could have been exposed and the only clinics open were filled with infected people. Going to one of them would be admitting defeat. All she could do was wait for Jay. Maybe he would have a plan; maybe they could both stay at the electric plant?

Standing up for the first time, her body was stiff, her skin raw and painful. She walked to the window and looked out, but couldn't see anything but light and globs of color through the plastic sheet. With a heavy sigh she paced back and forth on the cold tile, wanting to look in the mirror, but too terrified of how she would look. She did not want to see what she had become, what this outbreak was doing to her…no, she had to look. She only peeked for a second; the woman in the mirror was not her. The woman she saw could have come from Auschwitz. Putting her hand over her eyes to block out all images of herself a flood of panic rose in her. Eyebrows; eyelashes; hair she forgot to shave, Jesus, bed bugs could be hanging onto the strands right now.

Digging through the closet she found Jason's razor and quickly started at her brows. Her fear of seeing herself was now gone as she stared at her reflection watching her eyebrows disappear behind the razor. With her brows gone she rinsed the razor and looked at her lashes. Squinting one eye she tried to attack it with the razor to no avail. She was going to have to pluck them. Tossing the razor aside she grabbed her tweezers out of the medicine cabinet and leaned closer to the mirror. Grabbing five lashes with the metal prongs she pulled. Her eyelid stretched to an obscene length, her eyeball burning from the air hitting it. Using her free hand she pulled the lid back and the lashes snapped out. Her eye watered and stung as she blinked incessantly. Looking at the lashes she realized she hardly got a few. This was going to take a while…and it was going to hurt.

An hour later she lay on the floor with her hands over her swollen eyelids. She had finished twenty minutes ago yet the pain and constant blinking had yet to subside. Reaching down to itch her thigh, she thought about what she could put on to leave the house. She'd have to wear a trash bag. She didn't want to risk wearing a pair of Jay's sealed clothing. They could wear the bags and take the motorcycle up into the mountains; surely the bugs hadn't made it up there...man her leg itched. An itch. An itch? Even though she was flat on the floor she felt her head spin and vomit creep up in her throat. Maybe it was just a regular itch, it would go away in a few seconds...her arm itched too.

Jumping up she moved away from the floor as if it were the offender. Scratching her arm and thigh she wanted to run, to get away from the itching. Though she knew it was impossible. It wasn't something on her skin she could run from; it was something inside of her. *They* were inside of her.... It was too late.

Sitting on the edge of the tub, ignoring the two itching sensations, she looked at the gun. She and Jay had agreed that if they became infected they would just kill themselves instead of going to a shelter and being put down by the government. They said they wouldn't be hysterical and try to cut the bugs out like some of the people did, like Ashley did. Picking up the gun she set it on her lap and thought of Jay, she should wait for him., to say good-bye first. Although she wouldn't be able to hug him because one of the bugs could crawl from her to him. Then again she only had two itches, maybe she could cut them out? If there were just two, she could kill them or throw them out the window or down the toilet. She wouldn't have to cut deep and she had plenty of first aid supplies in the closet. She could do it, she could, she wouldn't be like the others who cut and cut because she only had two spots.

Putting down the gun she grabbed the razor that still had some of her eyebrow hair in it and cracked it against the sink. After three whacks and the help of the shotgun butt she freed the razor blade. Tossing everything aside she grasped the razor, being careful not to cut herself any more than necessary. The leg. The leg was the smart place to start, it started to itch first and she might need both arms to do it. Using her hand she found the exact spot on her thigh that was itching. It had a radius of an inch so she figured she should cut the whole spot out to be safe. Getting rubbing alcohol out of the closet she poured it over the spot and readied the blade.

Using the point she pushed the blade in a centimeter, the pain was intense but bearable. She pulled the blade back an inch, pulled it out, poked it back in and did the same thing making a right angel. The blood was pouring out rapidly now, dripping down her thigh and onto the white tile. The blade was getting slick with the blood. Her fingers slipped on the next cut sending the blade across her thigh in a jagged six-inch line. She screamed in pain, dropping the blade in the tub. The blood pumped widely out of her leg and the realization that she might have hit an artery set in. Instinctively she went to get a towel to stop the bleeding, but of course there wasn't any. Her hand over the wound was useless as the blood pumped out.

Even with all the pain she could still feel the itching sensation, she had to get the bug out. Picking up the blade she wiped it off on her non-injured thigh, held her breath and finished the last line to make the square cut. The cut was quick and hardly added any more pain to the area that was already on fire. With the square complete Jane smiled through the pain, she did it. Only what she didn't think of was that she still had to detach the meat of her leg from her thigh, this thought didn't come to her until she dug her nails into the slits and tried to pull the chunk out. Her fingers slipped off several times until she realized she had to slice more. Using her four nails she pulled back one side. The gap pooled with blood covering the yellow globs of fat. Dipping the razor blade in the pool she sliced over and over again in short quick motions. The pain wasn't as horrible but the sensation was making her want to vomit. Little by little the chunk pulled back until finally it popped out.

Holding the chunk of her leg in front of her eye, she tried to see if the little bug was in there. There was too much blood to see clearly. Standing up shot lightning bolts of pain to her thigh, looking down she saw her entire leg was covered in blood and that the bleeding was nowhere near done. Hopping to the toilet she tossed the chunk in, it splashed with a cloud of red. Hitting the flusher she felt confident watching the piece swirl around until it disappeared. It was a tiny victory, but she still had a long way to go. Now she had to stop the bleeding and get the one out in her arm before it moved.

Looking through the first aid kit she felt a bit woozy. Finding nothing to patch the hole (since they took out all the gauze; it was porous) she cursed her preparedness and popped a dozen aspirin. Then, after pouring alcohol on the wound she thought of an idea that would hurt, like hell. Fast as she could she took the cover off the light, squinted at its brightness and unscrewed it with her bare fingers. The tips of her finger burned and with each successive spin the smell of burnt flesh got stronger. Knowing she would need her right hand for the next surgery she used her left one and grabbed the red-hot bulb that had been on for hours. Without hesitation she crammed the head of the bulb in the wound. The sizzling noise was worse than the pain.

As the heat wore off she was thrilled to see that the wound was bleeding only a quarter as much now, though her left hand was going to be pretty much useless. After putting the bulb back to get hot for the next one she let her hand sit under the cold tap for a few minutes. It lessened the aching a bit but she knew the pain would last for days. Jane wanted to rest, she wanted to fall asleep, but she knew she had to cut the last bug out, then, then she could sleep and she'd live and things would get better.

Being impatient, not waiting for the last dozen to kick in, Jane took more aspirin and rinsed off the blade. Another pour of alcohol on the arm and she was ready. This time knowing what she was doing she was able to cut smaller incisions, not as deep. After the four cuts she realized she didn't have the extra hand to hold back the skin to cut it off, she was going to have to dig with the blade. With less fat on the arm it was a bit harder to cut through, but she did it one slice at a time until the chunk fell off. It was half the size of the one from her leg, if that, she just prayed that it was deep enough to rid her of the bug. Another flush and burn and she was done. Hardly being able to stand anymore she fell to the floor and slept deeply.

When she awoke she was insanely thirsty. After sucking down a dozen mouthfuls of water from the faucet she gasped for air and noticed the sun was almost down. She was alive and Jay should be home soon! Her energy was back up, it enabled her to ignore the pain and wait for Jay. Part of her wanted to race downstairs and wait for him, but she was terrified of leaving the bathroom. If another one of those got in her she couldn't handle having to cut it out. She'd wait in the bathroom, she'd tell Jason to strip down outside the door, to shave his eye brows and pluck his lashes before he came in, then when he came in she'd stay away from him, make him shower, douse him with bleach, then she could hug him.

It wasn't long after she awoke that she heard the motorcycle pull in. She was so excited she felt like a little kid, she would be safe soon. After the engine died she started to yell for her husband over and over again. She knew he wouldn't hear her until he entered the house, but she couldn't help but yell. Several minutes and her throat was hurting from the yelling, but it had worked, she could now hear Jay yelling back from downstairs. Seconds later she heard his feet pounding on the steps. As he neared her, her heart tightened, she raced for the door and locked it; she had to make sure he didn't have any bugs on or in him.

"Jane! What the hell is going on? Are you alright, let me in?" It was wonderful to hear his voice. She put her hand on the lock, wanted to let him in, but fear overpowered her love for him.

"I, I am fine. Ashley, she was infected; she tried to get in the house. I did what I had to do." She waited for a reply; she wanted to hear him confirm that what she did was right.

"You, you didn't get any on you, right?" His voice was soft and she could have sworn she heard scratching. Looking down at her wounds she decided to lie.

"No, no, I didn't. I came up here and scrubbed down. It's been hours and I don't have any itches, I'm safe. It's safe in here."

"Good, then let me in!" She stepped back from the door, his voice sounded mean, angry, as if he was mad that she wasn't infected.

"I, I can't let you in until you strip down and shave your eyebrows and eyelashes off." There was a thump against the door.

"Damn it Jane, just let me in! I'm fine, you know that."

"No, no I don't know that. I'm not letting you in until you do it Jay. I can't, I have been through a lot today and I can't risk you bringing one of those things into our safe room." There was pounding on the door now, he was furious, he was never like this, he had no temper, never yelled at her. Something was wrong, he had to be infected. Though if he was, wouldn't he want to protect her?

"Jane, for crying out loud, every second you keep me out here is a second more I have to get one on me. I'm standing on carpet you know, now, LET ME IN!" She started to cry not knowing what to do. Her hand instinctively went to her wounds. Cutting herself like that was the most traumatic thing she had ever gone through, no way, no way was she risking that, not even for Jay.

"I'm sorry baby, I just can't let you in, until you do that." There was that itching sound, he had them, she knew it. The itching was so loud; they were probably all over him. The door thudded. He was trying to get in; another thud.

"Stop it Jay, stop it! I can't have any more bugs get on me, I can't." She cried hysterically as she picked up the shotgun. The thudding stopped and the itching noise resumed.

"You...you have the bugs?" Jay's voice was soft, the voice she knew and loved.

"Had, had the bugs. I got rid of them, I cut them out. I'm fine now. You'll have to cut yours out before you can come in here...I can't risk you contaminating the safe room." Suddenly there was silence. For a moment she thought he had left, retreated downstairs to take care of his own bugs. Just as she was about to lower the gun there was an enormous thud. The door pushed in a bit, the hinges bending with pressure. Jane backed up to the window, she thought about breaking it out, climbing down and running, but the bugs were out there too. This, this was her safe place, the only place she was safe. She had to keep him out.

"Jay! Back up or I will shoot you!" The wound in her arm throbbed from holding the gun as she screamed. Her plea did nothing to stop the next thud against the door, the one that broke it in.

The door snapped off the hinge and fell sideways against the wall. Jay stood in front of her then, breathing heavy, his eyes red. He was naked, like he usually was after coming in from work. Part of her wanted to throw down the gun, to run and hug him, but his eyebrows. His eyebrows were not shaved.

"Baby, what did you do to yourself? Oh god." With his arms out he took a step to avoid the door just as Jane pulled the trigger.

The center of her husband's chest disappeared behind a red mist. He didn't fly back like in the movies; he merely stood there with a look of shock on his face. Jane watched as he wobbled and looked down at the flesh that was now gone. When the mist faded she saw the mess of meat, bone and organs. As he leaned against the wall and started to slide to the floor Jane was convinced she saw his heart beating inside the open cavity. It was that sight that made her realize what she had done, that the room was now contaminated. She killed him for no reason, she was going to get more bugs now, she was going to die, alone when she could have just let him in and they could have died together.

The realization was so intense that she put the barrel of the gun under her chin. The metal was still hot; it singed her jaw as she placed it just right. Without hesitation she pulled the trigger…nothing. Again and again and again she pulled it even though she realized that she had spent both shots the chamber held. The rest of the bullets were locked in a cabinet in the garage.

Tossing the gun aside she stood up, limped to Jay's body and gave him a light kiss on the forehead. She walked through the house and down the stairs like a zombie. Nothing was on her mind but getting the bullets she needed to kill herself. By the time she got to the kitchen she was exhausted. Her wounds were bleeding again and the pain was wearing her out. She had no choice but to sit down at the kitchen table. Pushing aside the cup of cold coffee that she was sipping only a few hours before, she put her head down. Just as her cheek hit her forearm she jumped up with a start as she heard a voice and cheering. It took her a moment to realize that her elbow had hit the television remote and turned it on. After all the silence the noise was unbearable, fumbling for the remote to shut it off the news report caught her attention.

On the screen the reporter looked thrilled, for the first time in months she was smiling while reporting the news. In a small box next to her there was a live shot of people cheering and the oddest part was they were outside. Jane stood up, shuffled to the television and put her face inches from it trying to focus on the report.

*To repeat, the bed bug epidemic has been solved! Scientists have found that a combination of two over the counter drugs will kill any and all bugs that get into your system. This is important news so listen carefully. If you are infected all you have to do is take the following two drugs and the bugs will die and be flushed out of your system in a matter of hours…*

Jane fell to the floor. She couldn't catch her breath as she heard what the two drugs were, because they were both in her medicine cabinet. Rubbing her hands over her hairless head she tried to remember where the key to the gun cabinet was.

# COTTON

"Sir…just take a deep breath, please just sit back down, breathe deeply. I know this is very hard, but…" Though his monotone librarian-esque voice trailed off, I did as he said with my hand over my face. Like anyone would, Tammy felt she had to apologize for my outburst.

"I'm really sorry my brother-in-law is just, well we are all a little…"

"No need to explain, in my line of business we see all sorts of grief expressions. Ranging from none at all to…well, rage." I knew he was talking about me, but I didn't care. Why should I, right? I kept my hand over my eyes; it was easier not to look at anyone. Much easier.

As I took the deep breaths I watched the pale thin man stand up through the tiny slit of my fingers.

"I'll give you a few minutes to compose yourselves. Then, we'll finish the matter at hand." With that he disappeared with no noise, like a ghost. I could feel the warmth of Tammy's hand on my knee; it started to rub up and down in a comforting, yet sexual way. I couldn't help but wonder for a split second, like I had so many times before, if she was as good as her sister was. Then I remembered where I was, what had happened. I put my frown back on.

I really wanted to remove my hand from my eyes but at the same time I didn't want to look at her. She was going to have that puffy look of grief sprayed on her face. I hated that look and I didn't want to see it because I never knew how I was supposed to return it. I tried the face out myself many times in a mirror. It looked good, I thought, but never real enough. Though I have never had anyone question my grief. Why would they? A grieving husband and father, anything is rational.

Tammy finally got the courage to speak; her words were spoken so gently that it seemed she was worried her voice could shatter me.

"I don't know what to say. I'm hurting so much...I mean, my sister, my niece. Oh god. I can't imagine what you must...be feeling." With that one hand moved to the back of my neck and the other farther up on my thigh. For a second I thought I might have a chance but then as she started to ball, I knew I didn't. Through snotty gasps she started to go on and on about how they looked.

"They look so amazing. Amanda, so beautiful and my Tina, Tina, she looks like a princess. She'd be so happy." That was when I had to speak up; I couldn't let her talk about how good they looked. They didn't! Not at all.

"Why does everyone feel they need to make comments about how dead people look? They look fabulous! Bull shit!" I stood up knocking my chair over and faced away from Tammy. I could hear her silent gasps of not knowing what to say. I waited a moment then started up my rant again.

"Amanda hated makeup. You know that! She would be pissed to be stuffed in a box with makeup on her face forever, like some goddamn clown..." A few tears shot out of my face, I was a bit surprised so I took advantage of them and lifted my elbow high in the air as I wiped them, making sure Tammy saw that I was in pain.

"I didn't mean to upset..." I raised my hand to show her to shut up as I darted to the window. Looking through the thick wood slats I could see the cars starting to pull in already, one after another. People sure love to show their support at a child's funeral. They always show up in droves like it's some sort of parade. The sick part is I bet that more than half the people that will show up never met the two of them. It's like they get off on this shit. Showing support my ass, they thrive on drama. They'll sit in the back and gossip and say "what a shame".

Getting my mind back on track I spoke up again.

"And Tina...shit Tammy...you know she hates pink! Fucking pink sparkles in her hair? She would be so upset at me for that...she'll never forgive me." With that I fell to my knees sending the blinds dancing with my falling fingers. Tammy ran over and placed her hands on my shoulders, I brushed them away and asked that she just leave me be for a moment.

I took my time getting up. Standing again I waited out the incident by looking at the mortician's license on the wall. It looked like a diploma from Harvard; only it was a degree on how to stuff a body. I started to think of what those sick bastards do for a living.

"Please...talk to me. You need to talk to someone. What is going through your mind right now?" From the distance of her voice I could tell she was sitting once again. This was good if she really wanted to know what was on my mind.

"Fine. I'll tell you. What's consuming me the most is stupid things. Things I never would have thought would bother me. Yet now they fill me with such a rage that I have no clue what do to... I keep thinking of cotton." I could hear Tammy mouth the word to herself not sure what I meant.

For the first time in a while I turned and faced her with my best grief stricken face and kept speaking.

"Cotton. I never thought I could hate an inanimate object so much. I hate it so much that I want to rip off all of my clothing and burn it. Because cotton is what is now sitting inside of my daughter's nose. Her tiny nose that I used to nibble on to make her laugh, which I cleaned just four days ago after she sneezed. I think of it crammed up my Amanda's nose as well. The nose that I gave countless Eskimo kisses to, like the one at our wedding…remember that?" Tammy started crying harder. She took my hand and I could tell she wanted me to stop, but I pressed on.

"It isn't only in their noses. It's in their ears as well. When you and I knelt between them a few minutes ago I wanted to whisper things I need to say to them, but I knew that damn cotton was also in their ears, so deep inside I knew they would never hear me."

"They can hear you…in heaven they can hear anything, even what's in your heart." Tammy was trying but I wasn't having any of it. Again I stood up, this time I made a backhand as if I was about to slap her but stopped at the last second and again retreated to the window.

"No god would do this to a three year old and her mother. No god!" Finally Tammy was silent. I carried on my rant.

"The worst? The worst part, the part that made me not sleep a wink last night?… The cotton that is crammed in between my wife's legs. The spot that made us one, the spot that gave birth to Tina. The thought of some man stuffing fists full of cotton between her legs made me throw up, twice last night."

"Why are you thinking of such horrible things? Focus on the good, the time that you *did* have them?" I ignored her comment and kept going.

"Tammy, someone, that wasn't family, saw my daughter naked. The thought of that alone makes me almost explode with a fury I cannot explain. Yet that isn't the half of it. To know that some man touched my daughter's naked body… to know that, that man stuck things inside of her, in places that should not have been touched for another fifteen years by anyone… that for eternity cotton will lie inside of my daughter, in every hole of her body until she rots…." I could hear Tammy get up.

"I'm sorry…I can't hear this, I can't do this. I know you're hurting, that you need to focus on something…but this?…I'll be out there." With that Tammy left the room in a hurry leaving me alone. I couldn't help but smile.

I knew I would only have a few minutes before one of the undertaker bastards came in to talk to me, so I took a swig of rum from my flask. Not that I wanted it, but I needed to have it on my breath so I could come off as drunk. Then I went about slapping my eyes to make them puffy and red. I had done this many times the past few days, works like a charm.

Hopefully I'll have a few minutes to relax before I had to put on my acting hat once again. Just a few more hours. I just had to get through the viewing and the funeral tomorrow. Then from there it would be just a few weeks of paper work, cashing the insurance checks and I could move on. I'll just have to give Tammy the whole, "I can't take living in the same house, same town" routine. Then I'll disappear and start the process over.

At first I thought the hardest part would be the killing, but I found that to be sort of fun. Then I thought getting away with it would be hard; yet it was easier than any TV detective show would make you think. This is the fourth time I'm getting away with this routine. The hard part? The hard part was getting away from these grief stricken idiots for longer than five minutes. That's where the whole cotton routine comes in handy.

# BLOOD SOUP

"Well you know what the old Italian women used right?" Carry said through a mouthful pretzels. She was on a diet so she ate low fat pretzels; the only problem was she ate three bags a day. Missy did her best to ignore the crumbs falling out of Carry's mouth and listen to her.

"It is so sick," she said swallowing, "they used to put their period blood in their spaghetti sauce!" That definitely got Missy's attention. She sat up in her chair with a disgusted look, not believing her best friend's story.

"No way, why would they do that? That is just disgusting." Carry laughed and took another mouthful before speaking.

"They believed that when the men ate the sauce they were consuming a part of them. In return they would be bonded to the women and faithful to them forever. I guess it was very common thing." Carry finished with putting another few pretzels in her mouth. Missy on the other hand was fascinated; she started to think deeply about what she said. In a way it was poetic, the man consuming the woman, making her part of him. The idea enthralled her; maybe it was just what she needed to make Chris take the next step?

"Anyway, you could always do that or cut off his balls." Carry snorted sending a spray of crumbs over Missy, snapping Missy out of her trance.

Missy's problems with Chris started from the day she met him. Being the fat girl, Chris never even noticed

29

her when he came in for his coffee every day. He'd always wait in Teri's line; even when Missy had no one in her line. Teri was beautiful; she couldn't blame him for wanting to be waited on by her. She noticed him every day though; everyday he came in she would stare at him and hope he would use her line. And one day, he finally did. Of course it was only because Teri was out. He was polite and friendly and even asked her a question, sadly it was about the whereabouts of Teri. Missy took the opportunity to lie and say she was good friends with Teri, that if he wanted to know more about her she'd be happy to sit with him on her break and talk. He gladly agreed.

The two chatted for a while and she did her best to keep the conversation off of Teri and to find out everything she could about him. When she lied and said that Teri was getting engaged soon Chris looked crushed. It was then she made the boldest move she ever had by asking if he would like for her to make him dinner some night, to cheer him up. When she asked, he looked her up and down and said, *sure*. That very night he was over her house. She made him a steak dinner, a real man's meal with potatoes. He seemed a bit awkward around her as if he was not sure if he wanted to be there. He was beautiful though, more beautiful than anyone she had ever been with, so she ignored it. And though she would never even kiss on a first date she threw herself at him; sleeping with him twice that night before he left.

Even though she knew he was just using her for a quick lay, she had never been happier. Not once in her life did she ever desire someone or something so much... and actually get it. It felt like a victory. She had won something. Only when he left her that night she wanted him back. She wanted to feel his warmth in bed with her. She didn't expect to ever hear from him again, even though she hoped she would. When he called the next day, she almost fainted. He asked if he could come over for dinner again and she agreed. The same routine applied, dinner, sex and he left. She offered for him to stay but he said he had to get up early to work, though he would say hi to her when he got his coffee. A promise he did uphold. When he came in he now went to her line every morning, he hardly even looked at Teri. Even though he was cordial and never showed a hint that they were sleeping with each other, she loved every second of the attention she got.

Weeks went by and he came over two to four times a week, the same routine always applying. She wanted to ask him to go to the movies or out to dinner or to even just go to his place but she was so afraid of scaring him away that she only made the vaguest of hints. Every night she did offer for him to stay and he would decline her with a kiss. She would then follow up the question with, *will I be seeing you tomorrow*, he always just said, *we'll see*. Never would he make plans ahead of time or tell her when he was coming. He would always just call by three in the afternoon and ask if he could come over. If it got to three thirty then she knew she would have the night to herself. On those nights off she would look up new recipes to make him, go shopping for ingredients and clean the sheets. Her life ended up revolving around those nights with Christopher.

For a long while Missy was content. She was getting sex regularly for the first time in her life; she had someone to cook for and someone to talk to at night. For though they had lots of sex, they also talked, during dinner, before sex and her favorite, the time between their love making sessions. It was then that she would lay, her arms wrapped around him, their bare skin touching that they would talk about their most intimate subjects. During the first month she learned all about Chris, every

31

aspect of his past and future hopes. Though not once did they talk about *them*.

It was near the end of the second month, when she was fully in love, did she dare ask about *them*. She merely asked what he thought they were. For a few seconds he didn't answer, and then he sighed as if he was dreading this conversation. In that instant she wished she could take it back, but it was too late, it was out. He went on and on about how he wasn't ready for a serious relationship, how he loved what they had and wanted to keep it that way for a while, that who knows what the future held. When she first told Carry about what he said she laughed and told her to enjoy it while it lasted. That he would leave her soon as he found a skinny girl. In the back of her mind Missy knew it was probably true, but she'd rather believe that *he* was in love with her too, that he was just too shy to face the truth.

The next month of their relationship Missy went out of her way to make Chris happy, to make him fall in love with her if he already wasn't. She added candles, then music to dinner. She brought toys into the bedroom and offered (and did) things she never thought she would. Chris reacted to it all with great pleasure. He would tell her all the time that she was amazing. Their relationship even grew to watching movies in bed together and…he even started to sleep over. This time, when she got the courage to ask again, he gave her a hard kiss and just whispered that he still wasn't ready. She wanted to explode emotionally. It was the next day when she talked to Carry that she learned about what the old Italians used to do.

That night when she arrived home she looked up what Carry told her and was shocked to find out that it was true. It was stupid and disgusting, but she figured she had tried everything else, might as well give it a shot, what did she have to lose? Her period should arrive in another day anyway. Chris still came over when she had it, of course she felt compelled to give him oral and in the second month they even started to have sex during it, something she never did before. So she knew he would still be coming over, her only question, how would she do this?

Always using tampons she knew that they would absorb too much of the blood and clots. Squeezing out one wouldn't do much, besides getting cotton tuffs in the sauce wouldn't do much for the flavor. A pad would be just about the same. What to do then? It took a while but she decided upon plastic wrap, baggies and string. It was unbearably uncomfortable the first day she wore it, but besides a bit of leakage, it worked. Twice that day she scraped the contents into a Tupperware container and rinsed off the plastic to make sure she got all the juice. For three days she did this until she had a solid three cups worth of her own fluid mixed with some water. It disgusted her having her own shed egg chunks floating around in Tupperware in the back of her fridge, but she thought of it as an experiment.

That third night she was ready to test out her ridiculous idea. She spent the afternoon making a homemade spaghetti sauce, she then carefully separated one portion size into another pan for herself (so she wouldn't have to eat her own blood, the thought of it creeped her out). With Chris's portion ready she tasted it and was satisfied that he would love it, she just hoped that pouring in her mixture wouldn't throw off the taste too much. With a deep breath she poured out the deep purple and red mixture into the sauce, it bubbled up in an odd way that made her giggle and gag at the same time. She spooned a couple spoons of sauce into the container, swished it around and dumped it back in the pot to make sure she got every last drop. After a quick stir she let the sauce sit to meld for a while.

When it came time to test the sauce she was nervous. Part of her just wanted to serve it and not have to taste it, but she knew that was stupid, she had to try it. After letting a spoonful cool, she took the tinniest taste she could. It wasn't disgusting, not at all, though it did have a funny iron after taste. Using a bit more spice and a lot more salt she got the sauce to taste just right, darn good in fact. Letting the pot sit, she got the rest of the dinner ready. She was nervous for a bunch of reasons. One, she hoped it wouldn't make him sick, she prayed he wouldn't notice anything wrong with it, but mostly, she hoped it would work. Even though she was realistic about it and knew that the chances of anything happening were astronomical, she needed that tiny sliver of hope to keep her going.

A quick few hours later and it was finally time. Chris arrived and gave her the usual kiss and ass grab before sitting down for the meal. As she plated the pasta they made small talk about their days. As she ladled the sauce on she did a small prayer in her head. Setting the plate in front of him she gave him a light kiss and hoped he didn't notice that she was acting suspicious. Sitting down with her "safe" plate she watched him intently as he covered the pasta and sauce with Parmesan cheese. She was glad for this; she hoped it would cover the taste even more. Holding her breath she watched as he twirled his fork around and lifted it to his mouth. He chewed like normal for a few seconds, paused, swallowed and then looked up at her.

"Is this a different recipe?" Missy felt as if she might faint. "Because it is delicious." She gasped with relief and shock. Her cheeks started to blush as she wanted to jump up in victory. Though it wasn't a win just yet, she had to see if it had any effect on him.

Taking slow, steady bites she could hardly keep down the food as her stomach did flips watching Chris eat. His mouthfuls got larger and were shoved in his face at a faster pace. He spoke no words, drank nothing and merely grunted with satisfaction as sauce splattered on his cheeks and shirt. It was as if he was becoming animalistic, it worried her a bit. Seeing the deep reddish-purple chunk on Chris's cheek she knew it had come out of her body. The sight of it dangling there, and the thought of him ingesting it, made her almost gag as she wondered to herself why she did this. Putting down her fork she thought about taking the plate away from him, but he was in such a rhythm of eating she didn't dare disturb him.

When Chris finished he threw down his fork, gasped for air and stared off into nothing. Missy had never seen him do this; she was scared and worried that she made him sick. With his sleeve he wiped his mouth stood up, blinked several times and finally laid eyes on her.

"Missy...I know I haven't told you yet, but I love you. I love you so much." Her heart dropped, then beat like a hummingbird's wings. For a second she thought he might have learned her plan, that he was doing this as a joke to tease her. When she didn't respond to his statement she saw his face cringe in pain. Trying to steady her breathing she sat still as he walked over to her, fell to his knees and wrapped his arms around her.

"I love you, I love you...if you don't love me yet, that is fine, I'll wait for you to be ready to love me. I'll do whatever it takes to make you love me." Missy couldn't speak. It was exactly what she wanted to hear for so long, but she just couldn't believe that he was saying it, that her sauce had *worked*. It made no sense. In a daze she suddenly felt his hands on her face followed by his wet lips cramming against hers. His mouth tasted a bit like iron. The thought of his tongue pushing bits of herself into her own mouth made her pull away and gag a bit. He was instantly worried about her health asking what was wrong over and over again until she answered.

"It's just…I have waited so long to hear you say that. It's hard to believe you are saying it now." He hugged her so hard a cough escaped her chest, followed by a long hard cry.

That night they made love, real *love*, not sex. Chris was a different man in the bedroom. His hands trembled as they went over her body as if her flesh was the most pleasurable thing in the world to touch. He held her, kissed her softly and whispered he loved her in her ear over and over again. After their third time, he stayed the night, not letting her go for more than a few seconds at a time to adjust positions. She awoke in the morning to the smell of bacon. Chris had made her breakfast in bed. He sang and giggled as he served her the tray. As she took bites, still not believing what was going on Chris massaged her feet and kissed her toes.

"Why don't we both call in sick today? I just can't stand the idea of not being with you the entire afternoon. What do you say?" He had pounced on the bed like a little child asking for permission. When she agreed, he jumped up, knocking over the glass of juice to give her a kiss.

They both called out of work for the next two days. They didn't leave the apartment once. They stayed in bed and watched movies, took showers together and made love in every inch of her apartment. When they ran out of food they called for take-out and giggled as they answered the door wearing nothing but towels. It simply was the three greatest days of Missy's life. Of course it had to come to an end.

Realizing they both had to work in order to not get fired they left each other that final morning with a frenzy of kisses. Chris was even holding back tears as he promised to come over the second after he left work and got some stuff from his apartment. During the day she received forty-eight text messages and five phone calls from Chris. Each one made her smile and blush with joy. Everything was so good she never even thought about what she had done to receive this love. She didn't think of how or why it worked and she didn't care. It worked and that was that, wondering why was messing with her luck. The only thing she did worry about was its affects, were they going to wear off and if so, when?

For a solid week Chris was stuck to Missy like one of those sucker fish she used to have as a child. It was wonderful, but at the same time she hated having him around for some things. Like when she had to go to the bathroom he wanted to go in with her. Which was horrible considering she usually didn't go to the bathroom with anyone in the house. Then there were the chores that were stacking up. The laundry hadn't been done, the dishes, dusting, vacuuming, she missed doctor's visits, hadn't grocery shopped, neglected her weekly visits to her mom and even hadn't showered alone since that first night. Part of it was heaven, the other part was getting a bit annoying. She needed some private time, but when she suggested it he almost started to cry. He said that if she loved him she wouldn't want him to leave for a second. Again, she didn't want to risk losing him so she kept her mouth shut.

It was in the third week straight of his suction that she noticed that the effects were starting to wear off. He wasn't as dependent on her. There were times where he would actually let her walk out of the room without following her. When he let her take a shower without joining her she felt relieved that he was easing up, yet at the same time she was scared that the spell would wear off and he would run for good. The feelings were conflicting her. Part of her wanted her space, but another larger part knew if he left, she wouldn't be able to handle it.

When the day finally came where Chris's face looked a bit blank and he stated that he was going to head home that night to catch up on some chores, Missy was conflicted. She made him promise to come over the next night for dinner, to which he agreed with a loving kiss. The silence in the house, the lack of hands on her body made her feel more alone than she had. It was an uncomfortable feeling that she avoided by cleaning the apartment from floor to ceiling. When she finished she took a long quiet bath and tried not to think. The silence and rest her vagina was finally getting was relaxing and welcome. In bed alone was a different story though.

For years she lay smack in the middle of the bed. Now after three short weeks she found herself always sleeping on the right side of the bed. Laying there alone that night she could not force herself to lie in the middle or on Chris's side. She had to stay on her side as if it was some sort of respect for her lover. Without the feel of another heartbeat, the warmth and touch of Chris, she had a hard time falling asleep that night. And just before she did fall asleep, she knew she had to collect her monthly visitor once again.

That next week was interesting. It was a mix of the two extremes. Chris still came over, though only three nights that week. And when he did come over he was surprisingly still lovely dovey. He gave her kisses, brought her flowers and even stayed over one night and told her he loved her before going to bed. It was perfect, it gave her the time to have her own life and still enjoy him at the same time. As her period arrived she was ready to decide to not give him another dose, but when he did not want to come over one night, she changed her mind. She didn't want to push it and put too much in this time, she probably just needed a bit to keep him going through to the next month. Who knows, maybe one more dose and he would be hooked forever. Not knowing how it worked in the first place meant there was no telling what would happen really.

The next day when she started to bleed, she once again made her contraption and collected the blood. On the third day of collecting she knew she had way more than she needed, but kept collecting anyway. Maybe if she got a lot she wouldn't have to collect it each month. Maybe she could store the mix in ice cube trays? That way whenever he seemed to go a bit awry she could drop one of those cubes in his meal and have him back in love with her instantly.

This time she waited until the flow stopped. Having collected every drop she decided to use just a bit, this time in a soup. That way, hopefully, he wouldn't get suspicious. In honor of the Italian ladies that gave her this idea she stuck with the Italian theme and made minestrone soup. Besides, she figured with chunks of tomato in it, any chunks of her would blend in. She hadn't made minestrone before so she followed a recipe she found online to the tee. Once it cooked for a bit she tasted it and added several seasonings to make it taste the way she thought it should. Satisfied with it, she pulled out a bowl for herself and put it in another pot. Then she lifted up the bowl of the red chunky liquid and steadied her hand to keep it from sloshing everywhere. The plan was to pour a few splashes in then pour the leftovers into a few ice cube trays. Sadly that did not happen. As the first plop of her mixture landed in the pot it sent up a splash of scalding hot soup that hit her hand. With a yelp, she let the bowl go.

Hands over her mouth she stood staring at the pot that now had an entire month's menstrual cycle in it, along with the bowl floating on top. As she stared, she sucked on the burnt spot on her hand, cursing her own clumsiness. Instantly she thought she should throw the soup away. As she turned off the burner she realized that all of her cycle was in it, nothing was left. She would have to wait another month to get more to feed him. That might be too long; she could lose him in that month. Without thinking she used a set of tongs to fish out the bowl, turned the burner back on and went about setting up for dinner.

After the soup simmered for a bit she reluctantly tasted it, spat it out and went about adding seasoning for the next thirty minutes until it was tolerable. She was nervous about giving it to him. It was a much, much stronger dose than the first time. If she had more time she would have made up another dish and given him only a cup full, but when the doorbell rang she knew that plan was out the window.

Chris seemed a bit cold, like he used to; kind and horny, but no emotion beyond that. He even looked a bit uncomfortable as if he was planning to break up with her. In fact, in the pit of her stomach she knew that was what he was going to do. She just hoped he planned on waiting until after dinner to do it. As he sat at the table with crossed arms he was silent. He was definitely trying to build courage. To distract him she rambled on about how amazing of a soup she made and rushed off into the kitchen. Standing at the stove she looked at the bowl that minutes before she thought was too big and switched it with an even bigger one.

At first Chris just swirled the spoon in the soup looking at it, clearly in deep thought. She wanted to ask what was wrong, but she knew if she did it would be his opportunity to make the break. Instead she had to do a counter attack and force the soup upon him. Shifting her chair closer she reached under the table and grabbed his crotch, leaned over and licked his neck. Then as he let go of his spoon she picked it up, got a heaping serving of the soup and seductively fed him. He was a bit reluctant, but he now had a silly smirk on his face and swallowed it. Clearing his throat a few times he blinked rapidly and spoke.

"That is good soup." Instantly he grabbed the spoon back from her and started to shovel it into his mouth at a rapid speed. Leaning back she felt cocky knowing she had won the battle.

Without another word he finished the bowl. Dropping it on the table he looked at her bowl and then to the kitchen door. With his spoon he pointed to the door and said one word.

"More?" Missy nodded that there was, realizing that she shouldn't have. Before she could even open her mouth to stop him he was through the door. Her legs were weak as she got up to follow him. Swinging open the door she gasped at the sight of Chris. His head was deep inside of the pot. Every few seconds he lifted it up, face covered in the cloudy liquid and chunks of vegetables and pasta, and gasped for air. Missy didn't even try to stop him. She just knew if she did she would be thrown aside. Instead she just watched in horror, terrified of how in love he was going to fall with her now.

When he lifted the pot to get the last drops she wondered if she should say anything. Nothing came to mind. The clattering of the pot on the stovetop snapped her out of her daze. Chris turned and faced her with an

41

intoxicated smile, his face covered like the loser of some weird eating contest. Without a word he stripped off his shirt, wiped his face off and then dropped his pants to the floor. Stepping out of them he walked over to Missy and scooped her up into his arms. She let out a tiny cry of fear as he brought her back into the dining room and dropped her on the table. Within a minute everything that was neatly set on the table was smashed on the floor, her clothing was off and Chris's head was between her legs. What he was doing felt so good she forgot about the situation.

After two orgasms her vagina started to become intensely sensitive. She tried to give him the sign to stop by clenching her legs slightly and tugging softly on his hair but he seemed not to notice. Instead he started to do an odd sucking motion. Normally it would have felt good, but she was starting to hurt. She whispered for him to stop, but he only grabbed her hips and forced his face deeper inside of her. His tongue reached depths of her body that no tongue had ever been able to. When he pulled back to take a gasp of air she took the opportunity and snapped her legs shut and turned to her side. Chris said nothing; he merely stood up straight and thrust himself inside of her. For the next three minutes she was slammed harder than she had ever been in her life. It was more pain than pleasure. When Chris pulled out and came on her side, she had never felt more relieved. Part of her wanted to curse him out, though she knew she was to blame for the sudden lust.

Chris seemed to calm down for a moment, but then he climbed on the table next to her and using two fingers to wipe up his semen, he thrust it inside her mouth. Normally she didn't mind a quick blast in the back of her throat, but this was disgusting. It was cold, thinning out and tasted strongly of iron. She gagged a bit, but went along with it hoping it would satisfy him.

"Jesus Missy! It fucking hurts loving you this much. I just, I can't get enough of you, I can't get close enough to you. I want to be one with you. That's it, we should become one, we should get married!" Hearing the word her father told her she would never hear if she stayed fat, sent electric tingles all down her body. Her mouth instantly said yes before she could process it. He kissed her hard, too hard, his teeth smashed into hers stinging her gums, yet he didn't pull back. He pushed his mouth harder on her until she couldn't breathe anymore. The only gasps of air she got in the next ten minutes were when he pulled back for his own minuscule breaths. It was torturous. She had created a monster that she couldn't handle and yet she couldn't wait to marry it.

Thinking of the wedding, seeing Chris in a tux and the faces on all her jealous friends and family was the only way she got through the next hour of touching, fingering, hard thrusting and oral once again. Parts of it were enjoyable, but mostly it was horrible. She prayed it was just that he overdosed, that it would wear off soon and then he would just be the guy he had been before. After he came for the second time and once again forced her to consume his seed, she suggested taking a shower, hoping it would calm him down. He was so consumed with kissing and licking her that even on the walk to the bathroom he didn't stop, making for an awkward journey.

In the shower he once again had sex with her; thankfully the spray washed away his semen before he could cram it into her mouth. When it was over and they were on her bed naked she thought he would start to settle down. She hadn't been with a man who could do it more than three times in a day let alone in an hour, ever. He should be spent. Pulling his mouth away from her breast for the first time since entering the bedroom he spoke in a quick stumbled speech.

"No, no, marrying you is not enough, not at all. I need to be in you, I need you to be in me. It's like, it's like I have this need to consume you. Think about it, my semen is inside of you, part of me is now part of you. Doesn't that blow your mind? Doesn't that make you feel wonderful?" By the time he finished his sentence he was straddling her, sitting over her hips, his dick hard and laying on her stomach.

"I really don't understand what you mean Chris. I think love and marriage are enough…don't you think? That is what most people do." Chris's face suddenly turned red, tears filled his eyes.

"Our love? Ours is not like normal, stupid people. No one, NO ONE, has ever loved someone the way I love you. And you love me that much too, right? Right? I know you do, you have to. I would die if you didn't." Missy was crying herself now too. She was scared. Chris was going insane, she caused this. If he got any worse there was no way she could fight him off. She didn't have an ounce of muscle and Chris had the body of a Greek god. Her only choice was to use talking to try and get his mind on a different track.

"Chris, baby. I have an idea! Why don't we get dressed and go look for rings and tell everyone we are getting married! It will be so fun." She did her best to say with joy and not fear. Chris leaned over, put his face in her neck and sniffed hard.

"Yes, yes, marriage, but first I need to be part of you, I need *you* to be part of *me*. Don't you see? If we consume each other, then we will become one, forever! It's the only way for us to guarantee that." Missy closed her eyes as she heard the deep voice so seriously next to her ear. She could feel his balls on her upper thigh and she wondered if she thrust up if it would hurt him enough to get away. She didn't want to hurt him though, not unless she absolutely had to.

"What do you mean by...consume Chris? You are starting to scare me." She whispered caressing his head trying to calm him.

"Scare you? Why on earth would I be scaring you? I want to be part of you...what is scary about that? Look, I'll show you." Suddenly he jumped up off of her and ran out of the room. Missy felt so relieved she didn't move fast enough to lock the bedroom door. Instead he was back in the room with a knife. With one shove she was pushed back onto the bed, he was once again straddling her, holding her to the bed, only this time with a knife in his hand.

"I want to feed you; I want to give you my life, like a mother would a child." His words were not making much sense and when he sliced a five-inch section above his left nipple she screamed. Blood started to flow out, over the nipple and down his chest. He leaned forward so the blood was dripping on her face. She kept her mouth shut and turned her face sideways as the warm liquid covered her.

"Drink from it, drink from me, of me, to be a part of me!" He screamed as if in pure pleasure. As the blood started to run up her noise she had to open her mouth to breathe. Doing so let globs of blood in her mouth, gagging her. As she coughed up the blood she watched it splatter on Chris's face. An odd smile had crossed his lips.

"Drink me in!" He said with glee in his voice. After swallowing several mouthfuls, having no choice as he blocked her nose, she felt as if she would vomit on his erect penis that was inches from her face. Thankfully he pulled away after the cut started to clot. She spat out his blood as she watched him sit back up and start to stroke himself, using the blood as a lubricant. He kept staring at her breasts making her fear he was going to cut her as well. She tried to move her legs a bit to see if she could now kick him in the nuts any better, but he was too far up, a thrust wouldn't do any good. Her hands were free though, maybe she should start to stroke him and then snap it backwards, that would give her the momentum she would need to push him off and run, but he would catch up if she did. She was fat and slow, he was lean and fast. But if she made it to the phone or the bathroom where she could lock the door she might be alright. Suddenly Chris's voice took her out of her planning.

"Did I ever tell you how much I love your nipples? They are so perfect! If we are going to be one, I should have one and you should have one." Before she could even register what he meant she felt a sharp pinch as his thumb and forefinger grabbed and pulled it out. Just as her hands grasped at him, the knife slashed right across the stretched skin, severing her nipple in one clear cut. As she covered her wound with both hands blood spurted out and mixed with the existing blood that was already on her. In shock she watched Chris look at the nipple he held in his fingers, kiss it and then pop it in her mouth. As his eyes shut and his jaw went to work chewing she turned her head and vomited.

"Stop doing this, please Chris, you are hurting me, I could die. If you love me so much you wouldn't hurt me…." She pleaded through the pain and tears.

"I know it hurts baby, I know, but it's the only way we can become one. By consuming each other we will be inside of each other. Don't you understand? We will mix our bodies and then we can attach them together. That way, forever we will be sealed together making one human. Our story will make Romeo and Juliet look like a school yard crush."

Missy took several slow, long, deep breaths while Chris kept mixing the two bloods that were on her chest into one mixture then licking it off his fingers. She needed to calm down so she could thrust him off and make a run for it. Gaining her energy she obeyed the fingers that pushed their way into her mouth and sucked off the mix of blood. It made her stomach churn more but she had to make him think she was going to go along with it before she made her break. As she started to count down from ten in her head Chris started to speak again.

"My balls! That's it! You need to eat one of them to have me in you!" Leaning back a bit he pulled his sac out from under him, squeezed it at the base to find both of them and lined up the knife to cut. Just as he was about to plunge it in she made her move and thrust her hips upwards with all her might. The motion sent the knife into his scrotum sac and then up and into his stomach about an inch. It also sent him off of her and onto the floor. Missy bolted up, took one look down to see two gray, vein covered eggs hanging out of what was once Chris's sac. His face was going white as his mouth gasped for air. She wanted to help him, to kiss his face and marry him, but at the same time she knew she had to run, so she did.

In the kitchen she grabbed the phone and started to dial the police when she suddenly realized there was no way she could explain the situation. That if she said Chris had been attacking her that he would go to jail. And if she told the truth, she would be put away in a mental institution; no one would believe her. Either way, she would never be with Chris again. The bathroom it was then. She could lock herself in there until the affects wore down, then they could get bandaged up and go and get married. It would all work out. She learned her lesson, never put too much in; she'd never do it again.

Just as she was about to reach the bathroom Chris stumbled in front of her. His face was sweaty and pale. His entire body was covered in blood and only one testicle was hanging out of the sac. Startled, she stopped in her tracks and looked at his hands, one had the knife in it, the other was a gray testicle. He was rolling it in his hand like some sort of stress ball, giving it a gentle squeeze every now and then.

"You...need to eat this, we aren't done yet...we are not one yet." Feeling exposed, being naked, she covered her breasts, her hand hitting her missing nipple with an absorbent amount of pain. When she looked down she saw that it was still bleeding, that her entire body was red. It made her feel sick and woozy. Little did she notice, Chris had taken the few short steps to her and was now right in her face. She wanted to scream, but a sudden wave of weakness washed over her body causing her to collapse on the living room carpet.

As the fog in her mind cleared, she thought about the blood on the carpet, how hard it was going to be to get it off, how when she moved she would lose her deposit. Then she realized that living was the priority. Getting her bearing, she realized Chris was kneeling beside her. He looked to be busily working. Seeing him snip a string with a pair of scissors, she realized he had sewn himself up, both his chest and scrotum. Patting her chest the pain was still there, but the wound was gone, replaced by a thin line of thread and swollen skin. She couldn't believe she had been out that long, that she didn't wake up as he'd sewn her.

"Oh, good, I was so worried about you my love. Here take a sip of this." Propping her up, he brought a glass to her lips. Maybe it was over, maybe it had worn off and he was coming to his senses. Being parched she greedily took a large sip of the liquid that she assumed was going to be water. Instead it was thick as a milkshake with hard chewy chunks. It was warm and tasted of blood, meat and ice cream. Not being able to stop the swallowing instinct, a good gulp went down her throat. The rest she spat up and coughed.

"What…was…that?" She managed to get out between gags. He brought another cup to her lips, this time she kept them sealed until she saw that it was water. This she drank greedily.

"Well I figured it might be hard for you to chew a raw testicle so I put it in your blender with some ice cream and milk. It's not that bad, you should give it another taste." Missy started to cry as she lay there, naked on the carpet, blood dried and flaking off her stomach. Guilt started to wash over her. This was all her fault, the man she loved was going to be scarred and deformed the rest of his life because of what she did.

As she cried, Chris stroked her hair with a worried look and hushed her with a cooing noise.

"Chris…we need to get to a hospital. We need to get treated. Then we can get better and get married. I know that is what you want right?" Chris stared at her, his eyes were not the ones she knew so well. They were crazed and seemed to look through her. She could tell he still hadn't come down.

"Missy, Missy, Missy, marriage is so fake! That is not love; love is not a piece of paper and a ring. It's being one with each other; do you know how few people *really* become one?" Missy closed her eyes and sobbed, knowing she was going to have to fight him off if she was going to survive this.

"Chris, baby, what else do we need to do to become one? You have consumed me and I have consumed you. What more is there?" She figured if she could get him to speak, to tell her his plans she could use that knowledge to make her escape. As she finished her sentence she started to suddenly feel tired. As she sat up a bit, he offered her some more water, which she gladly accepted, finishing the whole glass in a few gulps.

"You don't have to worry about anything else we have to do. You are just going to take a nap, so you will feel no pain; I will do all the work. When you wake up, we will be one...forever." Not being able to hold herself up anymore, she laid back and fought to keep her eyes open.

"What did you do?" She heard herself say through a sleepy slur.

"I crushed up some of your sleeping pills and put them in the water. That way when I use the needle and knife you won't feel it. Now I love you baby. Jesus! I wish there was a word stronger than love...now go to sleep, when you wake up...you'll never be away from me.... We will be one." His voice echoed off into her dream as she slipped away from the world.

Sharp, burning pain that covered Missy's entire body woke her. Opening her eyes she saw the bedroom ceiling. She could feel the weight of Chris's body on top of her, his penis inside of her. His weight was making it hard to breathe or move. Shaking him caused waves of agony throughout her body and it did nothing to wake up him up. In fact his body felt a bit cold. Lifting her head she tried to see what he had done, how he had made them "one". Where their chests touched she could see a hard plastic stretched between their skins. Using the one arm that she could move she tried to separate them and realized he had poured super-glue between their bodies. She screamed as she thought about how painful it was going to be to separate them. Little did she know it was much worse.

Craning her neck more she started to say *no*, over and over again. Everywhere their skin touched had been sewn together. He had used thick shoelace string, lacing it into his side, down into her side and back, all the way down their bodies ending with their feet tied tight together. Looking at the other side she saw that it was the same, only on this side his hand was in hers and a large nail went through both palms keeping them sealed together. Putting her head back down, she stopped crying and stared at the ceiling. She felt weak and knew she was still bleeding in dozens of places. As she calmly summoned her strength to start screaming she prayed that someone would find them before she died and truly became one with Chris forever....

# THE MAN AT THE END
# OF MY BED

Every night I wake up and an old man is standing at the end of my bed. If I wake up my wife to see him, he disappears. If I turn on the light, he vanishes. No matter what I do, he is there, every night, watching me sleep.

It started the first night my wife and I slept in our new home. We were hardly unpacked, boxes were stacked up everywhere and our mattress was on the floor. Exhaustion had set in around ten. It was a long drive and a lot of unloading that day, but my wife and I were happy, we were finally in our first house. Carla and I had been married almost two years and the last year of it was spent in my parents' basement saving up money to buy this house. The joy we had when our family left us that day was unparalleled. We chased each other around the house, made love in half a dozen rooms and finally flopped on the bed to sleep.

Carla always amazes me by falling asleep in less than forty-eight seconds. I haven't even finished adjusting my pillow by the time she is snoring away. That first night was no different. As she was snoring, I was tossing and turning. I opened my eyes and stared at the ceiling for a minute, curious if I should turn on the fan, I slept better when it was cold. As I propped myself up I had the fright of my life. Standing at the foot of the mattress was man. It was dark, but I could tell it was a person. My heart slammed. Normally I slept with a baseball bat under my bed incase anything like this ever happened. Not being unpacked, I had nothing, not even a lamp to turn on to see what this man looked like.

I swallowed hard and slowly sat up, the man didn't move. I desperately wanted to wake up Carla but I was afraid that if I did, the man would attack. I was naked and had no weapons, he probably had a knife or worse. Wetting my lips and finding courage, I whispered.

"Take what you want...just leave us alone, alright?" No answer, no movement. That made me even more nervous. I figured he was some sort of a sicko. He was going to tie me up, rape Carla and make me watch. I moved my leg slowly out from under the blanket, hoping that I could get some footing and maybe lunge at him before he could attack us. Maybe I could wrestle him long enough for Carla to wake up and call the police. Frustratingly, the mattress was on the ground, which meant getting up was ten times harder than normal. I decided to take a different route.

"Look, I'm going to get up slowly. I'll show you which boxes have the valuables, you can take them and I won't call the police, I swear." No answer. I felt tears bubbling up in my eyes I was so nervous. As I stood up awkwardly, the man didn't move, not even when I revealed that I was naked before him. I decided it was time to make a move... I dove right at him. As I leapt, I squeezed my eyes shut and tried to think of defensive moves. *Go for the eyes, groin and throat, they are the most vulnerable, at least I think.* Instead of slamming into the man's body, I felt myself falling and then hitting the ground with a force that shot the wind out of me like a rocket. Rolling over I quickly got up, figuring the man moved when I shut my eyes. When I looked around, I didn't see him. I only saw Carla getting up frightened, yet groggy.

"Did you trip honey? Are you alright?" I ignored her. There were too many boxes in front of the closet for him to have gotten in there, he had to have left the room. Flicking on the light I raced for the door; bathroom, guest room...nothing. Racing downstairs I grabbed a lamp from the living room for protection and darted around the floor, only to find the alarm was on and all the doors and windows were shut. Lowering the lamp, I heard Carla calling me from the top of the stairs.

"Mark! Mark? Should I call the police, what is going on?" When I looked up the stairs, I saw she had the sheet wrapped around her, one hand on her chest and another holding her cell phone. Shaking my head I walked up the stairs as she kept asking what was wrong.

"I...I thought someone was standing at the end of the bed? I got up and dove at him." Carla's pixy features frowned.

"Did you check everywhere? Is the alarm on?" I told her there was no one in the house. That I must have been dreaming, even though I knew I was wide-awake.

"Maybe it was a shadow or something. It is a new place, you're not used to it yet."

"Yeah, maybe, let's go back to bed... I'm sorry I woke you." As we lay back down in bed she gave me a kiss and started snoring thirty seconds later. As for me, my adrenaline was racing like it had never done before. I was wired and wide awake. I snuck out of bed and dug through boxes until I found a flashlight and my bat. With both of them next to me, I slept fitfully.

The next day we got our bed put together and pretty much finished unpacking our bedroom. Being the only room that was fully done, we ate Chinese food in bed and watched a DVD since we didn't have cable yet. We didn't talk about the incident in the morning; I figured Carla had forgotten about it being that she was half asleep. She had done that before, had full conversations with me in the middle of the night and then forgot all about it the next day. Yet as she piled some General Tso's on her plate, she asked me about it. I was a bit embarrassed about the whole thing, having no clue what it was myself so I just brushed it off as a dream.

We cleaned up our mess, made love, this time in the empty dining room and then went to bed. That night I shut the bedroom door and made sure my bat and light were at hand. I felt safe and comfortable enough to sleep. I have a small bladder; on a normal night I wake up anywhere from one to three times to take a leak. That night was no different. We had gone to bed at eleven and I had woken up at one with a full bladder. Half asleep I threw back the covers, started to get up and froze. I felt someone was there, at the end of the bed.

Turning my head I saw the figure again. I felt a chill wash over my body as if someone had dumped ice water over me. I looked to the door and saw it was shut. I'm a light sleeper; there was no way anyone could have opened the door without me noticing. I closed my eyes, rubbed them and told myself to wake up, wake up. When I opened them I let out a gasp as the figure was still there. Keeping my eyes locked on it I reached for the flashlight, brought it in front of me and snapped it on. To my horror the figure lit up. It was an old man. He wore a red flannel shirt. He was slightly hunched over and bald. Liver spots, wrinkles and a hooked nose covered his face. White tufts of hair sprouted out of his ears and nose. He stared at me for a spilt second… then disappeared.

I swore the man in front of me was real. He was not an apparition, he was not see- through or wavy like they always show ghosts in movies. In fact, the flashlight lit him up; the light did not go through him. I sat still, not moving the flashlight not believing what I saw or knowing what to do. I was in shock. A twinge from my full bladder finally pulled me out of my daze. I got up slowly, searched the room, under the bed and in the closet with my flashlight and found nothing. I took the bat and the flashlight to the bathroom with me. I peed with the door closed and my back to the window. I was spooked to say the least.

Back in bed I kept the flashlight gripped hard in my hand. I tried to tell myself that it was just a dream, that I had twice now, but I didn't believe it. The hard part was I didn't believe in ghosts so I had no clue what was going on. Besides, even if I did believe in ghosts, the house was only five years old. It wouldn't be haunted, couldn't be. I didn't sleep the rest of the night. When Carla woke I didn't tell her a thing, I was embarrassed by this thing that I couldn't explain.

We unpacked most of the boxes that day and a few friends came over to have a small house warming party. We got a few cute decorations and a nice candle with one of those diffuser covers that make it have a light glow. Carla liked it so much she put it on the bureau in the bedroom and lit it as we got ready for bed. I felt a bit nervous getting undressed as two nights in a row I had a disturbing visit. I did my best not to show it, but Carla sensed something was wrong. She massaged my shoulders lightly and told me to go to bed. I went to get up and blow the candle out but she told me to leave it, she liked it flickering. Honestly I liked it too, though it wasn't much, it made the room more visible, even if it did cast creepy shadows.

Amazingly I fell asleep, probably because of the lack of sleep and the aid of a few too many beers. Of course too many beers meant I was going to have to wake up more than usual to pee. That night I woke up around twelve, having only gone to bed a half hour earlier. I was still a bit tipsy so I forgot about my friend as I got up. It wasn't until I took a few steps and was face to face with him did it all come back to me.

His nose was only a few inches from mine. I could feel his warm stale breath on me, he was real, I knew it. The candlelight flickered, lighting up his face. I could see every wrinkle and detail. I could now see his eyes were probably once a bright green, though now they were a milky green, like creamed spinach, as cataracts now clouded them. I blinked, but didn't move as I looked at his face. He did not move either, only his eyes, they scanned over my face just as mine went over his.

"Yooou." His voice hissed, it was low, gravely and weak, yet his mouth did not open as I heard the words.

"Who are you, why are you in my house?" I whispered. As much as I wanted to shove him and call the police my arms were pinned to my sides with fear.

"YOU." Again his mouth didn't move. The voice was still gravely, but this time, much louder. I wanted to look at Carla to see if she had awoken to see her husband face to face with an old man in her bedroom, but I couldn't look away. Suddenly his head turned and looked at the candle; I looked at it to see why it had drawn his attention. The second I turned to it, the flame blew out and a small dark stream of smoke came up. When I turned back to the man, he was gone. I was broken from my trance. I swung my arms widely, dove on the floor, looked under the bed and raced out of the room. I searched the house again, this time with a flashlight and as quietly as possible. I found nothing.

That night I did not sleep again. I formed theories about how a man lived in the attic; he had secret passages that he slipped in and out of without being noticed. He may look old, but he must have been spry to be able to move so quickly. I had heard stories like that before, people living in your house without knowing about it. It was the only explanation.

When Carla woke up that day I made a lame excuse to go in the attic, something about wanting to check the insulation. She said to be careful and started to unpack dishes as I climbed up through the small hole on the second floor. I took my bat and flashlight with me, not that I would have room to swing the bat in the attic, but it made me feel better. I peeked my head up inside, not knowing if it would get cut off or not. Thankfully, it did not. The attic wasn't finished so when I got myself up inside I had to do my best to sit on the rafters to not fall through. I could tell in an instant that there was no one living up there, no secret passages, yet I still crawled around, sweating and getting dirty. After checking each corner, pushing on beams hoping a magical passageway would open, I gave up. I sat, my butt hurting on the small beam, and cried.

My parents lived an hour away. I tried desperately that night to talk Carla into going back to their place to get a few "things" I forgot. When she asked what I had forgotten I stammered and said some old memorabilia stuff in the basement. She gave me a look and said they could bring it up next weekend when they came up to help us paint. She then asked me what was really wrong. I was embarrassed, how could I tell her? I couldn't think of a logical explanation and I didn't want to sound like a fool or worse, have Carla think I was nuts. I told her nothing was wrong, that I missed my parents and that this was all new to me. She gave me a kiss and told me I would get used to this, after all, this was our dream house.

When Carla went to bed that night, I decided to stay up and watch television, I wasn't tired, or so I told her. I waited for about twenty minutes and then snuck upstairs and listened for her snores. She had an awful big snore for such a small woman. From the sound of the snorts I knew she was sound asleep. I took my flashlight and bat and got my laptop. I then sat in the leather chair in the corner of our room that looks at the bed. Being in the corner, it was the perfect spot to observe. While I waited for this mystery man to appear, I looked up ghosts online, even though I refused to believe it was one. I read scores and scores of information. None of it seemed to be relevant to what was going on here. The room didn't get cold, the image didn't disappear with light, it spoke and looked at me. Very few stories said anything about that.

After three hours of reading website after website about spirits I started to get droopy. That was when I put my Mac to good use. I turned on the web cam, hit record and faced it away from me, at the bed. I set it on the little table next to the chair and fought off sleep; though it didn't work long. Before I knew it, my neck was hurting. I woke up and looked across the room to see the time, but I couldn't see the clock, it was blocked... by him. He was back. Glancing at the computer I hoped it was working and I got up.

I could feel the freeze of panic starting to come over me again, but this time I wouldn't let it. I fought it off as I trudged across the room. His back was to me, he was staring at the bed again. It was the perfect opportunity. The plan was to shove him in the back, see if he would move or if my hands would go right through him. I took a few deep breaths, approached, and just as I was about to shove him, I heard the voice again.

"You..." The man didn't move yet the voice was in my ears. It was all around me. The words locked me up instantly. Inches away from him I could not for the life of me bring my arms up to him. Then, as if someone else took over my body, I took off my shirt, walked past the man, and got into bed. I pulled the blankets up to my chin and looked at him. For the first time I saw him move. He simply nodded at me, as if he approved of me getting into bed. As he stared at me I felt my eyes get heavy... and I fell asleep.

In the morning I woke, not scared of the man for the first time. It was as if he put some sort of calm over me. I was awake before Carla but I could tell she was starting to wake up. I propped myself up on an elbow and watched her rise. She was beautiful. Seeing me, she pulled the covers over her head; I pulled them back down and hugged her.

"I have to tell you something." She gave me a look that said "go ahead" as if she wasn't sure it would be bad or good. I told her the whole story about the man at the foot of the bed. I even got up and grabbed my laptop. I fast-forwarded the recording to the correct time and the screen went white. I smiled, not surprised he wouldn't let me get him on tape. Carla being an IT specialist grabbed the laptop and tried to figure out what had happened. I simply told her it was him. She was skeptical the rest of the day and kept asking me if I was teasing her. I told her I would wake her when he came again.

Around two that night he was there. I nodded to him, but he didn't move. I looked to Carla as if to ask him permission, again he didn't move, this time I knew it was alright. I shook Carla gently. She woke not remembering why I was going to wake her.

"Don't be scared." I whispered as she sat up. Seeing the old man she let out a wail and reached for the lamp. I told her to leave it off, he liked it that way, though I didn't know how I knew that.

"Who is he? Why is he here? I, I don't get it." I wrapped my arms around her.

"I don't know. I just know he is here to stay." I held Carla tight as we stared at the man. After almost twenty minutes he turned and started to walk away. As he walked, he dissolved into nothing.

For weeks we searched records and old papers to find out if a man died in our house or on our land to no avail. There was nothing anywhere. Night after night he appeared, sometimes he would say, "You", other nights he would say nothing. A few nights I saw him almost smile and once I even saw him scratch his head. But regardless, every night he was there, for how long each night and at what time, I never knew. He didn't seem to go by a schedule, he showed up when he wanted and just watched us sleep. At first, Carla wanted to move, but then somehow, he calmed her just like he did me. We learned to ignore, or more so, live with him.

For a while, Carla wouldn't make love with me in the bedroom, but after a few months, she had no problems with it as he never appeared until after we went to bed, no matter how late it was. We both wanted to give him a name, but we never could agree on a fitting one, so we just called him *the man*. For some reason, we never told any of our friends or family about our nightly visitor. It wasn't that we were afraid of not being believed, it was more out of a respect for him. We didn't want to disturb him. Most people would have brought in a ghost hunting team or tried to get rid of him, but for some reason, he became, sort of… family.

Shortly after a year of living in our house, Carla and I woke in the middle of the night hearing the man's voice booming in our ears. "YOU, YOU, YOU" over and over again. We both jumped up, alarmed at what was going on. He didn't move, he just stared at us like usual, yet the word kept repeating louder and louder in our ears. Almost instantly, I knew he was trying to warn us of something. Jumping up I ran around the house to see what he was trying to tell us. When I got to the living room, I wasn't surprised to find the couch was on fire. Within seconds I had put it out by using the kitchen fire extinguisher. It took a while for the fireman to figure it out, but what happened was the outlet behind the couch shorted out from a faulty old lamp wire and the fact that the couch was pushed too hard against it. They said we were lucky, that another five minutes and the house would have been in flames. The chief even asked me how I knew it was on fire. I lied and said I came down to get a snack, he said it was the luckiest midnight snack ever. The next night Carla and I stayed up to thank the man. He didn't respond, but we knew he heard us.

Over the years, there has been almost a dozen times he has woken us to alert us of something. From small things like over sleeping for a flight, to when we had our first kid, he would wake us up to let us know our baby wanted a bottle. As our family grew, we introduced our kids to the man and they grew to love him as well. He never looked different, never spoke any other words and never changed the look on his face, yet I felt like I knew him more and more as every year passed. We came to love the man so much; we decided we could never leave the house.

It's been eleven years since we moved into the house and there hasn't been one night we haven't seen him... and I hope there is never a night I don't see the man at the end of my bed.

# DEAD LOVE
## (Inspired by True Events)

Everyone had big hopes for Ani, even her professors at cosmetology school. They all said she was the best makeup artist they ever saw. Ani was going to make it someday; she was going to be one of the few lucky ones who actually made a living, a good living applying makeup. It was Ani's dream to be a makeup artist, a dream that would come true, only in a way she never thought possible.

When her parents died in a suspicious house fire, Ani found herself broke and out of money. They had never been smart with their money, donating major chunks of their income to the church on a weekly basis. Having no insurances and nothing but debt to leave to her, Ani was forced to get a job to support herself, to save up to make that move to Hollywood. The small town in Iowa didn't have any of those fancy department stores where you could go and get a liberal paint job on your face for a free sample. The only job involving makeup, was the one Ani took; *Makeup Artist for the Deceased* at the local funeral home, The Waving Corn Resting Place. Ani took the job the day she graduated from cosmetology school.

At first it terrified Ani to be near dead bodies. After the owner, Mr. Dillard, showed her the ropes the first week and she applied makeup to the first body, an elderly woman with so many wrinkles it was like filling in the Grand Canyon with foundation, she relaxed. Still, the first month she refused to be alone in the basement. Then, slowly, but surely, she started to enjoy the company of the dead. They didn't complain about the makeup, they didn't move and smear mascara or blush the wrong way. And part of her felt good about making someone look beautiful one last time.

For the first year, she still did living people's makeup on the side. As she started to lose her tan from being in the basement all day, her patience for yapping faces stopped. Her lifelong dreams of moving to Hollywood started to fade as well. So much so, that when she finally saved up enough money to move there, she used it to buy a condo within walking distance of the funeral home instead. Before she knew it, twelve years had gone by. It didn't matter though; she found her true calling and her one *real* love in life.

Ani never had many friends, her parents wouldn't allow it. Over the years at the funeral home, the few she did have, slipped away. It was a slow process but the living started to annoy her. They complained about everything. Fussed and fiddled with things they shouldn't and made the world a horrible place. It got to the point that Ani even threw her television out. She just couldn't take the complaining anymore. Just like her parents... nag, nag, nag. Telling her she wasn't good enough, forcing her to read the Bible for hours at a time, locking her in the prayer closet when she misbehaved. The worst was when her father gave her his special punishments, the ones that he told her to never tell her mother about. Talking people, anyone really, reminded her of those miserable days. She liked her life now, the quietness, the calmness. Just Ani, the body, soft classical music and her makeup.

When it came to dating, Ani never had a boyfriend. Again it was on the sinful list growing up. The one time she kissed a boy in junior high, her father saw her. It was a kid that lived down the street. They hid in the backyard. Somehow her father had found them and saw the kiss, her first and only kiss. His eyes filled with such rage that the boy wet himself when he approached him with a stick he picked off the ground. Her father swung at him too, but the boy got away. Ani never talked to him again, mostly because her father gave her extra special punishment that night, telling her over and over again in her ear that no man, beside himself, was good enough for her.

After he died, she was talked into going on a few dates. She wasn't bad looking, plain in all aspects, but not nearly ugly. It was awkward dating. She didn't know how to act around men. Because of this they found her odd. When they found out what she did for a living, they never called back. Ani quickly gave up the whole dating thing. Mr. Dillard and his family still try now and then to get her to go out with someone, but she always finds an excuse not to.

As the years ticked by she got used to a comfortable routine. Wake up, eat breakfast while reading a book (she replaced TV with books, most people thought she was even odder not knowing what finalist got booted off of American Idol, but she didn't care), head to the funeral parlor and see who was there to make up. If there was no one she would usually just sit in the basement with her books. Waiting, hoping, someone would die, so she'd have company.

When a body did come in, Mr. Dillard would introduce them to Ani.

"Ani, I'd like you to meet Mr. Patrick. Died today at the age of 45, heart attack while in the cornfield. Shame, I'm almost twice his age." Every time a body came in it would be some variances of that. Always a Mr.

or Mrs. followed by a first name, age and cause of death; as if it was important for her to know when she put on the makeup. Ani would even sit there while the body was stripped naked, stitched up and embalmed. She enjoyed watching the process and even learned to do it herself. In a way she considered it a transformation, like a nasty caterpillar into a beautiful butterfly. The loud, foul person was being drained of its nastiness, becoming something wonderful.

At times Ani would help with the dressing of the body and moving it from table to coffin. She did all sorts of odd and ends that were not in her job description, which she was fine with, as long as they kept her in the basement, away from the grievers. Ani would do anything to stay away from them. Only when absolutely no one was around would she go into the parlor. And even then it was usually for a touch up before people arrived. At the first sounds of someone coming in she would scurry away like a mouse back down the hidden elevator that brought the caskets up. This was the way life was. That is until one particular body came in.

Ani arrived in the basement at her normal time. She was giddy to see a body on the table; it was still in the morgue body bag, so it had just arrived. In fact she could even hear Mr. Dillard saying goodbye to Marv, the meat wagon driver, as he liked to call himself. Ani hated him; he disrupted the bodies and was a loud mouth that never shut up. Anytime he came into the basement she would make an excuse to go and hide until he left. She was more than happy to have missed him today.

Like always, Ani felt a bit of anticipation upon the arrival of the body. Who would it be? What would they look like? Would it be damaged? Was making them up going to be a challenge? She wanted to take a peak but calmly waited until Mr. Dillard came down the steps still laughing at some lame joke Marv had just told him.

"Top O' the morning to you Ani!" His usually greeting, which Ani just returned with a smile and the occasional wink.

"Let's see what we have today, shall we?" She knew that was her cue to get up and assist him moving the body out of the bag and onto the embalming table. She was excited to see who was in the bag, for some reason, more than usual. Her heart sped up as if she knew someone special was inside. Ani would later say that was how strong their connection was, that she knew he was the one before even seeing him. As Mr. Dillard grasped the large zipper and pulled it down, Ani could feel her breath being taken away.

"Ani, I would like you to meet Mr. Mike, 39, his wife poisoned him. A shame. She almost got away with it too. They only did an autopsy because a family member requested it. So sad." Ani heard the words, but they were slow to sink in, for she was struck instantly by Mr. Mike's face. Not that she had ever seen him before, she hadn't. Instead it was just like in the movies, love at first sight. She felt it instantly and she knew he did too. He had to of, one of his eyes rolled open and stared right at her when his head fell to the side from being moved onto the table. It was almost as if he winked at her. Her heart started to beat fast, her hands started to sweat. Finally after all the years of being alone, she found a true love.

Mr. Dillard went about his usual chatter as he began the embalming process. Ani on the other hand did not go about her usual routine of going through her makeup and agreeing with whatever he said. Instead she just stared at Mr. Mike. She wanted to hold him, to climb up on the hard cold table and wrap her arms around him, to warm his body. She was going to have to wait though, until he was ready. Mr. Dillard hardly noticed she was staring so intently and even if he did she knew he wouldn't say anything anyway.

As she watched the blood leave his body through the small tubes, she started to love him even more. It was almost as if he was being purified, cleansed of all his human evilness. That without the hot blood coursing through his body he could be everything he was not in this life. Perfect. Ani went on watching; only looking away when Mr. Dillard looked up at her with a small smile.

After a while Ani helped dress Mr. Mike. Occasionally she did this and other times, if the person was too big for her small frame to lift, Mr. Dillard's son would help. This time she jumped at the opportunity to do so. With the suit neatly in place Mr. Dillard spoke the magic words.

"Well, all done here Ani, time to work your magic. Good looking guy, no deterioration to the face. It should be a rather simple day for you. Let me know when you're done and we'll box him up." Ani didn't move an inch until a solid ten seconds after the upstairs door shut. Alone at last, she exhaled deeply and walked over to Mr. Mike.

"I thought he would never leave." She giggled in a whisper to the stiffening body.

"I saw the look you gave me. I feel it too. Amazing isn't it? It feels…it's, it's just amazing." Ani was at a loss for words with these new feelings. Instead of speaking, she slowly walked around the long table, gently touching his pants and shirt as if she were trying to seduce him. She wanted to speak. She wanted to open the floodgate of conversations she had deprived herself of over the past years. To tell him everything, to let him get to know and understand her, yet they wouldn't come out. In time she told herself, in time.

Mr. Mike's eyes and mouth were sewn shut and all of his orifices stuffed to help stop leakage of the formaldehyde. This didn't bother Ani; it didn't make Mr. Mike any less of a man. All she had to do was simply snip the stitch and slip the thread out to open up his eyes. She'd then be able to gaze into those beautiful eyes.

"Don't worry. I know it's uncomfortable. But I'll take the stitches out soon. You'll be just as good as before. We just need to get through the next two days without suspicion. Then, then we'll be together forever; just like we want." Ani spoke this half out loud and half in her mind. For she knew he could hear her either way, their connection was that deep.

"I'm going to make you so beautiful. Your family…." Thinking of Mr. Mike's family, of his friends stung Ani. It was like tiny little darts hit her in the ribs. She didn't want to think of Mr. Mike alive, with, with assholes. She didn't want to think of him speaking and acting like one of them, because he wasn't like them. At least now he wasn't. She tried to brush it off, telling herself that his past was merely that, a past. Besides it only existed to get him to here. He was hers now and that is all that mattered.

"You like classical music Mr. Mike? Why am I even asking you, of course you do!" Cheering herself up Ani put on her favorite Bach symphony and got to work with her makeup.

Every stroke of the brush, every pat of the sponge and every dab of concealer was done with more love and care than Ani knew was possible. Not only was she making him up to look good for the wake, she was making him perfect for their…their honeymoon. Of course over the next few days she would have to reapply it, but that didn't matter, you always had to start with a good base.

"I know you're not used to makeup and that you think guys shouldn't use it, but let me tell you, you look incredible with it. Uh...not that you need it all! It just makes you look even better." Embarrassed at what she had said Ani leaned over and gave him a light kiss on the cheek. She could feel her own cheeks flush with excitement. It was the first time she had kissed anyone in years, it felt good to finally share, love.

When Ani finished the makeup her job was done for the day. She called down Mr. Dillard and together they put him in the coffin Mr. Mike's mom picked out. It was a cheap one. Ani was angered that anyone would show such disrespect for Mr. Mike. She did her best to hide her feelings though, besides he wouldn't be in it long.

Together they brought Mr. Mike upstairs and placed the casket in the holding room. A small, hidden, refrigerated compartment that kept the bodies cool while not on display. It was the usual routine. They would place him there, then tomorrow, before the showing they would wheel him out and let him thaw a bit so there was no moisture on the casket. Ani would then do "touch ups" to make sure he looked great as they put him on display along with all the flowers that usually poured in from all over.

Ani had explained to Mr. Mike before wheeling him up that he was going to have to stay the night here, but not to worry, in a few day's time they would be together forever. Besides, she needed the time to get her apartment ready for Mr. Mike and to figure out a plan on how to get him back to her place without anyone noticing. That was *not* going to be easy.

At home that night Ani went to town cleaning her apartment. Every nook and cranny was dusted, polished and dusted again. She organized her classical music CD's into alphabetical order, she figured Mr. Mike would like that. She even emptied out her fridge to prepare it for the shopping she was going to do, Mr. Mike ate healthy stuff, she would too now. Don't want to disappoint him. Ani even cleaned out drawers and closet space for him. He needed a place for his clothing, clothing she was going to have to buy along with the new food.

When everything in the apartment was in full order she sat down, exhausted. She hadn't done that much work, ever, in her apartment. It looked great and she just knew that Mr. Mike would approve, heck he was going to love his new home. It was still early so she had time to make it to the Super Wal-Mart to do some shopping. First she bought some nice cozy outfits for Mr. Mike, then it was off to the food aisle. She had a bit of trouble picking stuff out, but she finally got a ton of healthy food that would be just right. *It had to be.*

At home Ani unpacked everything. She put away the groceries with labels facing out because Mr. Mike liked it that way, and then folded his laundry putting it away in his newly cleaned out drawers. Everything on this side was set. Next she had to plan on how to get Mr. Mike home. She sat on the couch, which had just been fluffed, and thought. The hard part was going to be getting the body out of the casket in the short time between the morning viewing and the funeral. If she could somehow distract Mr. Dillard long enough to pull his body out and hide it in the funeral home she would be all set. Filling the casket with cinder blocks would not be hard at all. And no one would open the casket after the last viewing; they never do. Besides, she could activate the sealant on the box so they couldn't. The problem was she wasn't strong enough to lift him.

Throughout the night she wrote down over a dozen different plans, scratched them out and wrote a dozen more. Finally she came down to one that seemed like it would work. When the family exited to the cars Mr. Dillard and two ushers would quickly take all of the flowers out of the room and put them on the flower car. Then, the two ushers would stand at the door with the pall bearers to give them instructions while Mr. Dillard and Ani removed all the jewelry the family requested to keep and closed and sealed the casket. Then they would wheel out the casket to the bearers. It was during those five minutes that she was going to have to pull this off. First she would have to plant six cinder blocks in the elevator, which would be the easy part. Then, just as the ushers leave she was going to have to rush upstairs and tell Mr. Dillard that the drain was backing up again. She was going to have to plug it and wet the floor to make it believable. Now, even though the body would need to be on the hearse in a few minutes he would attend to the emergency. If the drain backed up, it would fill the room with blood and force the home to shut down for three days to be "sanitized." It was when he went down to take care of the drain that she would have to tip the casket over, let Mr. Mike drop to the ground (she'd make up for it later), drag him onto the elevator, put the blocks in place of him, seal it and then wheel the casket out.

While everyone went to the church and graveyard she would be left alone in the home like always. She could then go and get the wheelchair they kept in the front hall for elderly guests, pull Mr. Mike up into it, wrap a blanket around him, put some sunglasses and a hat on him and race across the street to her apartment. It would be daylight out but the street was quiet and she should be able to get him into the apartment and get the wheel chair back before anyone noticed it was gone. Thinking of the plan, going over every single detail in her head made her exhausted. She slept well that night and dreamed of Mr. Mike and how it would be when he was home with her.

The day of the plan she did her best to act normal. Mr. Dillard did asked once if she was alright, she brushed it off as the start of a cold. After that he didn't ask her again. While everyone was upstairs she plugged the drain and sprayed water into it and all over the floor, at this point her heart was racing and she felt a light sweat start. When she was summoned upstairs to do the closing she raced to Mr. Dillard and said she was trying to clean and the drain started to back up. After a long list of curses he told her to take care of Mr. Mike while he tried to unplug the drain. It was all working. Seeing Mr. Mike laying there looking beautiful she talked to him in her head, telling him it was all going to be alright soon. Just as she was prepping to push him over she heard a sniffle behind her. It was Mr. Mike's mother.

"I...I just need to say goodbye one more time." Ani thought she was going to pass out, she was so close to getting caught.

"Uh...ok, but please Miss, be quick, we have to get him to the church." The next three minutes were torture as the fat woman caressed Mr. Mike's face, dripped tears onto his suit and kissed his forehead a dozen times. Part of her wanted to feel sad, but jealousy of someone touching her man was making her angry.

Mr. Mike's mother finally left after some young man came and got her. Ani looked around to see if anyone was coming, she was safe, but had way less time than she needed. Without hesitation she dumped the body on the floor, dragged him to the elevator and tossed in the bricks, carefully placing cloth in-between them so they wouldn't clack together. After a quick seal she sent the coffin out and prayed everyone would leave in a matter of minutes. Thankfully after Mr. Dillard told her the drain was all right, but to keep an eye on it, everyone left. The silence of the funeral home, knowing she was alone with Mr.

Mike, that she did it, gave her a feeling she never had before in her life.

Within twenty minutes Mr. Mike was propped up in her recliner and the wheel chair was returned back to the funeral home. It was done. Her fairy tale ending was happening. She would be with the love of her life forever....

When she arrived back that night Mr. Mike was right where she left him, listening to music.

"Honey I'm home! I hope you got a good rest after all you have been through." She said as she took a seat next to him, placing her hand on his cold one. It was then that she realized that his eyes and mouth were still sewn shut. She gasped to herself, darted for her scissors and rushed back.

"I'm so sorry love; let me get those for you." With a few quick snips she had pulled out the thread that was lacing his left eye shut. Seeing his beautiful green eye she smiled and giggled. The next eye was a bit more difficult; she had to tug harder than she wanted, apologizing the whole time. On the last tug the upper eyelid tore open on the far corner. She gasped, screamed and hugged the body, slowly rocking him to ease his pain. After kissing it better and drying her tears she went about carefully, very carefully cutting the glue from between his lips. With eyes looking at her and his mouth open she leaned in and gave him a full hard kiss, their first kiss. Swirling her tongue around his mouth, sucking on his lips she made sure it was one of the best kisses he had ever had. When she pulled away and saw the look in his eyes, she knew it was.

The next hour she spent cooking a big dinner while music played. In between each chop and slice she would run over and kiss Mr. Mike on the lips. Her mouth also didn't stop either. She talked and talked telling him her whole life story, her darkest secrets and her deepest fantasies. She opened up to him like she never had before. It was a glorious feeling for Ani. Her head ached with joy as she wished she had this feeling much earlier in life, but she knew that was impossible, because it was Mr. Mike who brought it out in her.

When dinner was ready she lifted Mr. Mike up by sticking her arms under his armpits and pulling, she plopped him down in her computer chair and wheeled him to the dinner table. After lighting a half dozen candles she shut the lights off and turned the music up a bit, Bach of course. She ate slowly, blushing as she chewed, self-conscious and nervous of what Mr. Mike would think of her. She wanted to make a good impression after all. Looking over at him she knew he loved the massive steak she had cooked for him, hers tasted great and his was the better piece, it must be delicious. There wasn't as much talking during dinner but she figured it was because both of them were nervous. Besides it was more fun giving each other the sexy looks they were exchanging. As dinner continued, the talking went down to almost nothing, as they both knew they were going to end up in the bedroom after she cleared the plates. The anticipation was intense.

Before she knew it, Ani was in the bedroom with Mike (she dropped the Mr. by the end of dessert according to his pleading for her to be more casual). She played a CD while he lay in bed and she got changed in the bathroom into a silk nightgown she bought earlier that day. She had never worn one and felt silly in it, but she knew he would like it on her. When she did her best to walk seductively back in the room she was shocked to see Mike had gotten naked and was under the covers.

"Well that is awfully forward of you." She said with a giggle.

"True, I guess I am being forward myself. Guess we'll just have to keep going like this." With that she crawled onto the bed, on top of him and kissed his lips. Trembling, with her gut doing flips, she proceeded to kiss his neck, chest and work her way down his body. By the time she reached his crotch she was amazed at how into it she was. She never had much interest in men or sex, but now it felt like all those years of doing nothing, of touching no one, was coming out of her. A dam of lust was bursting and she was going to ride the wave. Without hesitation she took him in her mouth. It was all new to her, but it seemed so natural, she knew she was doing it right. Listening to Mike moan with pleasure, confirmed this. After a few moments she made her way back up to his mouth.

With a few soft kisses she reached down, no longer trembling, grabbed him and forced herself down onto him. It was a mixture of pain and pleasure so profound her mind went blank as her body thrust harder and faster. When it was over, when she felt a burst of heaven through her body, she lay next to Mike, holding his body tight to hers. The cold of his body sent a tiny chill down her rapidly cooling one, but it was nice. She whispered she loved him in his ear and she heard him saying it right back to her. It was the most perfect moment in her life.

They made love twice more that night. The third time they tried to do a different position, but with Mike's inability to move it was awkward and didn't work. He apologized profusely but Ani refused to take the apology for there was nothing to be sorry for. In the morning she made them breakfast in bed. It was more food than she had cooked in years, especially since she normally just ate oatmeal, but she wanted to impress him and it seemed to do the job, the smile on his face was priceless. When she reluctantly left for work (after a quickie) she left Mike in front of a stack of books with plenty of snacks and drinks.

When she arrived a few minutes late to work, Mr. Dillard gave her an odd grin.

"I have never seen you with such a blush before…if I didn't know better I would think you had a date last night." Ani couldn't help but have a giggle fit.

"Oh my goodness! The Misses will be so happy to hear this news! Who was the lucky young man?"

"A lady doesn't kiss and tell!" And that was the most she would reveal, even after he went and told his wife Bonnie, who then came running down the stairs and greeted her with a hug followed by a procession of questions. She merely answered that he was the perfect man, a gentleman and that they would be together forever. Bonnie quickly told her to invite him over for a family dinner. Ani brushed it off as too quick and Bonnie agreed saying that after two weeks though, he *had* to come over, no excuses. The rest of the day was filled with smiles and hurried work, as she couldn't wait to get back to her man.

When she arrived home the apartment was filled with an awful smell. Instantly she knew what it was, but not wanting to embarrass Mike she decided to go about it discreetly.

"Honey I'm home!" She said having always wanted to say that line (or more so hear it). She leaned over Mike from behind and gave him a dozen kisses on the head while trying not to breathe through her nose.

"Why don't we take a bath honey?" The thought was seductive, it turned her on, but at the same time she knew it was necessary to clean up the mess and address the situation. When she finally got him in the bathroom she undressed him slowly, trying to turn him on at the same time as trying to find the leak. With his shirt off she kissed his chest covering up a gag with some moans as the stench was getting unbearable. When she started taking off his pants it was right where she hoped it wouldn't be. His anus had lost its stuffing and formaldehyde was leaking out at a rapid pace along with chunks she didn't want to see. The sight and smell of the goo made her start to cry. She apologized to Mike and finally admitted what was wrong.

"Don't worry baby, you are just a bit sick. I'll take care of you though, I will. I just need to get back to the funeral home to get some...medicine." With a quick kiss she hurried out of the room wiping her eyes and leaving Mike naked on the toilet seat.

On the short walk across the street Ani almost had a breakdown. The road was deserted like always, yet for some reason she froze right in the middle; exactly half way from her apartment and the home. These odd thoughts started to come from the depths of her mind. They started to tickle her conscience, teasing her about reality. They said things like *what's wrong with you* and words like *corpse, dead body* and *cadaver.* The words swirled around her mind, kept her frozen there, scared and confused. The thoughts dug deeper into her mind until she realized Mike was dead, which she of course knew, but for some reason the words hurt her. They were disgusting and upsetting. For a split second she thought of getting rid of Mike, there was still time to get away with it, but then his smile came into her mind. The smile warmed her thoughts, covered her brain in happiness and pushed out the bad images.

It wasn't until a horn startled her did she realize she was sitting in the middle of the road. The fact that she was there, headlights beating down on her scared her to death. Getting up she scraped her knees on the gravel, muttered sorry and raced for the funeral home's back entrance. She wasn't too worried about making noise when she entered; the Dillard's slept in the far front of the house and wouldn't hear her. She was confident she wouldn't get caught, that was until she opened the door and found Mr. Dillard sleeping on the prep table. Having flicked on the light she wished she had used a flashlight, for Mr. Dillard's snoring burst into a grumble as the lights awoke him.

"Who's there? What's going on?" If Ani didn't know his voice she would have thought a corpse was rising from the dead as he sat up with the white exam sheet over his head. When he pulled it down he saw her and calmed down to the point of embarrassment.

"Sorry Mr. Dillard, I uh…thought I forgot a CD here that I was looking for. I didn't mean to…wake you."

"No bother, not your fault, you would have no clue I would be in here anyway. This is embarrassing really. The misses and I got in a fight and so I, well I came down here to cool off, guess I fell asleep." Ani felt confident that he wasn't going to ask her any more questions as to why she was here. She was safe, but she didn't know how to get the material she needed without raising questions.

"I should head back up, the couch would be more comfortable than this slab, sort of makes me feel bad for our clients!" Mr. Dillard got up and started to walk away when he suddenly sniffed and turned back to look at her. She froze not realizing what he was doing as he put on his glasses and looked at her. This made her look down at herself and realize she was covered in formaldehyde goo. Before she could think of an excuse, before she could wipe it off and laugh and make a joke, Mr. Dillard was inches in front of her examining it, knowing exactly what it was.

"What have you done my girl?" He said to her in almost a whisper. She started to feel her breath leave her lungs; the thought of losing Mike was unbearable.

"It's…uh…" She gasped out not knowing what to say. The thought of saying that it was from earlier in the day flew through her mind but she knew it wouldn't work, instead she said the truth.

"Please…I love him…please don't take him away." The tears flowed freely from her eyes. It felt good to say it, but the fear of the response outweighed the relief. Mr. Dillard stepped back from her, wiped his mouth, took off his glasses, rubbed his eyes and took a seat by the small desk he usually ate his lunch at. Ani just stood there, frozen, not sure what to do, if she should run and take Mr. Mike with her, be outlaws running from authority or if they should pull a Thelma and Louise and drive off a cliff together.

After a few moments of watching Mr. Dillard bite his nails she went and got the few handfuls of water proof gauze and sealant she needed, stuffed it in her pockets and went back to the same spot she was standing in for so long, waiting Mr. Dillard's decision.

"It's the good looking bloke isn't it, the one that got poisoned?" Ani could only nod and stare at Mr. Dillard who hardly looked at her.

"You can't keep him forever you know. He'll just keep seeping all over you and in time he will decompose and stink up your place. It will be a mess and you'll end up in jail with real criminals for doing something stupid. Is that what you want?" Ani nodded no, licked her lips and spoke.

"But we love each other so much, he is the nicest guy I ever met." Tears came out of Mr. Dillard's eyes at her response.

"Ah, love…. You need to let him rest where he needs to be. Look, I'll give you tonight to do something about it, after that I can't help you. You'll get caught sooner than later and I won't be able to help you then.

You'll lose him regardless and you'll go to jail, I don't want that for you, you are too good of a girl." Ani was hearing what he was saying, though the words bounced around in her head in a fragmented way that refused to acknowledge the fact that Mr. Mike was dead and that she had to get rid of him. Instead she heard what Mr. Dillard said as *Mr. Mike is no good for you, he'll leave you and hurt you, you should get rid of him now, before he hurts you.*

"You don't understand, Mike would never leave me, NEVER! He loves me and I love him more than anything in the world, we are meant to be together." Mr. Dillard's face crumpled and turned a bit red, just as she felt hers getting hot.

"Dearie, you are not making sense. Mike is dead; he has no thoughts or feelings. He is rotting in your apartment. I'm trying to help you, hell I could get in trouble for not turning you in as it is. I'd lose my license and go to jail for helping you, but I'm willing to do that for you because you are good kid." Again she heard the words, but as they bounced around and reformed they sounded angry to her; *Mike is no good, you better leave him or I will make you leave him! Do you understand me?*

"I will do no such thing Mr. Dillard! Never, ever, ever!" She screamed with all her might. Her body started to tremble and she felt a tickle of heat and anger wash over her. Suddenly she knew what it must be like to be a mother who had to protect her young, or a lover protecting their love.

"Oh dear…. We better get you some help Ani, I don't think I can help you myself." She watched him sit back down, rub his face once, sigh and pick up the phone. As she saw his pudgy finger hit the first number she knew she had no choice but to stop him. Spinning around she opened a sterile drawer and took out the large stainless steel bone knife that was used to cut through bone to "reform" an accident victim for a viewing. Without thinking she took four steps toward Mr. Dillard, swung the knife down and cut the phone cord. At first that was all she thought she would do, but then she watched her hand as if it were someone else's. She watched it lift high and swing down onto the bridge of Mr. Dillard's nose. The crack and splat was sudden, but beautiful. The scream was not. Mr. Dillard put his hands over his broken, bleeding nose. The screaming had to be stopped, so she watched the hand swing the blade down again, this time sideways, right into the open mouth. His cheeks split open with the ease of cutting paper, when it hit the back of his throat, she saw his tongue had split open and cords of veins and flesh snap in half until the blade hit something hard just an inch away from cutting clean through. She pulled the blade back out and raised it again, but it was not necessary. Mr. Dillard fell to the floor, gurgled and spurted a few times before falling silent.

In less than two hours Ani had drained Mr. Dillard's blood, pumped him with formaldehyde, stitched him up and given him an ample layer of makeup. In fact he looked better than he ever did. She couldn't help but smile as she held up a mirror for Mr. Dillard to see himself.

"See how good you look!"

"By god! I taught you well. I look marvelous. Thank you dear Ani, thank you, thank you!" Ani could feel her cheeks blushing, she was happy again, especially now that he understood what was going on finally.

"Ani, dear, be a doll and get the misses for me would you? Bring her down and give her the works like you did for me. She would love a great make over." Ani thought about it for a second.

"You really think so?" He assured her she would so she picked up the bone knife and headed up the stairs to the house. Though she had only been to it once she knew exactly where their bedroom was. When she arrived the door was open letting her hear the low snore of Mrs. Dillard. Creeping up next to the bed the old woman didn't stir at all. As Ani raised the blade she thought of hitting the old lady in the face but thought of how much work the mister was, all that stitching made her fingers hurt, so instead she went for the throat. Once again the blade cut so smoothly, that the woman died without even opening her eyes.

As she finished Mrs. Dillard's makeup, making her look like a movie star, Ani started to worry about Mike, having left him home alone and naked for so long, he must have been so worried, but she had to finish up here before she could go back. After a quick conversation with Mrs. Dillard about how good she looked and how she couldn't believe she never let Ani do her makeup before, Ani cleaned up the rooms. Helping them get upstairs was hard but once they were in the living room snuggling on the couch she knew the Dillard's were happier than ever. With a quick hug and kiss to each she hurried off back to her man, exhausted.

When she got back she found Mike slumped on the floor in a pile. He had slid off the toilet, landing half in the tub, half on the floor. Ani started to cry with guilt at the sight of him, it took her almost fifteen minutes to get him up and even then he had lost a tremendous amount of fluid through the hole she still had to plug. During all of this, Mike was silent except for grunts of disapproval; he wouldn't even answer her apologies. By the time she got him dressed and into the bed he was so angry he wouldn't even respond to her advances, not even when she went down on him. Frustrated she rolled over on her side of the bed and cried.

"We can't live like this!" Mike finally spoke. She was worried about the comment but thrilled that he was speaking again.

"What do you mean? It won't happen again, there was an accident, I told you, I'm sorry I left you alone so long."

"No, you can't take care of me like this forever, I will get worse, you know that and you could get caught and then where would we be?" Ani thought about it, as much as she wanted to ignore it, she knew it was true. By tomorrow morning people would notice that the Dillard's had changed. Before she knew it they would come after her and find out the truth, then they would take her away from Mike… she couldn't let that happen.

"You are right. What do you suggest then?" She rolled over and wrapped her arm around him.

"That you join me, then, then we'll be together forever."

"Okay…you are right."

By the time she and Mike arrived back at the funeral home the sun was rising. Ani worked quickly knowing that anybody that died over night would be brought in around nine in the morning. With Mike sitting in the blood covered chair watching her, she filled each of her orifices with the gauze and sealant; it was unpleasant to say the least. With all the orifices plugged except for her mouth, she kissed Mike and told him she loved him.

"Ani I love you, that is why you are doing this, so we can be together forever." After that Ani swallowed a dozen pain killers and sealed her lips together, she could only get a bit of air through the cloth in her nose, it was hard but enough to live. Lying down on the table, she cut a small incision on her ankle and inserted the blood draining tube. As she watched the crimson fluid flow away from her, she felt relieved that it was leaving her body. The cut on her neck was harder to do and hurt more, inserting the formaldehyde tube and feeling the cold goo pump into her was horrible, but she knew in a few moments she would be with Mike forever. Looking at the mirror she smiled as big as she could, for she was beautiful, for the first time in her life her face was made up with elegant and perfect makeup.

Michael Gore

## EARTHQUAKE PREVENTION
## (Inspired by True Events)

"Ah man, ah man!  It's worse than I thought, this is bad.  Bad, bad, bad."  Herbert kept examining every inch.  His hands were covered in gunk, flecks of grass and tree pollen sticking to the wetness of his fingers.  He had to find out how much was there, and man there was a lot.  A lot more than he thought was possible.  How could this be?  He pulled the rubbery tube closer to his face; the tree branch it was dangled over came with it.  "So much pollution.  It's in every inch of her."  Wiping his hands off on his pants he walked away from the woman's intestines he had strung up in the tree to examine.  Feeling defeated, and walked over to her.  Standing over the twenty-four year olds body, Herbert started to yell.  Telling her how much pollution was in her body.  The corpse with its various stab wounds and sliced open, now empty stomach, said nothing, but Herbert kept yelling at her.

"I have to save California and no one even cares!  Do you realize that by killing you I prevented another earthquake?  I'm saving this damn country. *Jesus,* it's all so polluted."  Frustrated and nervous of the work he had ahead of him he got back into his car and drove off.

Two weeks later, Herbert was pleased that there hadn't been an earthquake.  He knew one *was* coming, but he was keeping it at bay by killing.  It was working well so far.  Though he was saving millions of lives with these

86

murders, he still thought it would be a good idea to confess his sins in a proper format. Arriving at the church, he contemplated to himself that if California made it through till 1973 without an earthquake then he should get an award of some sort. It was already November so he didn't have much more to do to get them through the year.

The church was rather empty, being the middle of the day and all. He was never one for going to pray, but never questioned God or the work he was doing for him. There was no priest in the confessional; he had to wander around until he found one cleaning a stained glass window towards the back. He asked if he could confess. At first the pudgy priest with graying hair told him he'd have to come back during confessional hours. When he saw the look on Herbert's face, he changed his mind. The priest pointed the way to the boxes on the far wall for them to head to, but Herbert declined saying that he was fine to talk out in the open. The priest nodded and urged him to confess.

Herbert stood staring at the stained glass window. It started to quiver a tiny bit, but he ignored it and told the priest about the young woman he had recently killed and the bum before her. The priest's face was void of expression, he only said "go on". When Herbert looked back to the window he saw it trembling some more. He knew an earthquake was about to happen.

"You see Father, you see? Look at the window, look at it, it's shaking. An earthquake is going to happen. I have to stop it, oh, oh how sorry I am, but I have to stop it." As the priest looked to the window to humor him, Herbert stuck a four inch steak knife into his back. Twisting it back and forth made the man scream too loud. He covered the man's mouth, pulled out the knife and stabbed him over and over again until he was silent and on the floor. Putting the blade back in his pocket he ran to the window, put his hand on it, it was still. Herbert was relieved. He'd saved the millions once again.

A few months and twelve bodies later, Herbert was still saving California. The last time he killed, he used a gun and shot four boys at once. He figured the four polluted bodies would hold off a quake for some time, but he never knew. He never knew how long the last murder would last or how long California would be safe for. Sometimes it would last a month or more, other times, not so long. With four of the polluted out of the way, he figured he'd have a break for a while... sadly, his break only lasted three days. While driving home one day he passed an elderly Hispanic man weeding his lawn. At first he didn't think anything of this man, but as he passed by, his hands started to tremble and shake. *God, no, no please, another one... really?* The shaking got worse, they shook so much he had to pull the car over. *Ok, fine, fine.* As Herbert yelled out loud, his hands stopped shaking.

With a quick u-turn, Herbert was driving back towards the man doing yard work. Stopping his car he grabbed his rifle, jumped out and walked a few yards to the man who had his back to him. Lifting the rifle, he could see there were people all around him, witnesses, but he had to do it, there was no choice. With one quick pull of the trigger, the man was on the ground. Back in the car, Herbert drove away calmly as the witnesses watched and made note of his license plate number. His hands were not shaking anymore; once again, he had saved lives. When the cops pulled him over a few minutes later, he tried to explain he was saving so many with the few he took, but they wouldn't believe him. He told him they would be sorry, they would be sorry.

At his trial Herbert told the world how his thirteen victims were polluted. That killing them saved California for some time and his bloodshed is why there had been no earthquakes in such a long time. A month after his imprisonment California had their first earthquake since before his killings. Herbert knew it would happen. The second he felt the rumbling, everything came back to him, the horrors that he was preventing with his killings. He was barely five years old when it happened. His father had just put out a cigarette on Herbert's arm. Even at five, he knew that crying more would just cause him to get another burn or a hit or worse…. Letting the tears stream silently, he hid under the kitchen table. All he could see was his mother's beautiful ankles in light pink heels, his father's dirty boots, the broken glass spread across the floor and the meatloaf that was still steaming sitting in between all of it. Hearing more yells, Herbert scooted back as far as he could and grabbed the edge of the table cloth for comfort.

The rumbling started after the third slap Herbert heard. Being only five and never experiencing anything like it, he had no clue what was happening. The room started to shake, the floor trembled, the table above him suddenly slid away, leaving him exposed and able to see his mother holding onto the counter top, his father doing an odd dance in the middle of the room, trying to stay on his feet. Herbert screamed over and over again for his mother, as the shaking picked up, all she could do was scream for him to not move. He didn't want to listen to his mother; he wanted to be with her, needed to be with her, that was his only safe place, in her arms. As he tried to stand up, he got knocked to his feet by a violent tremor. Seconds later, the old linoleum floor cracked, it started under his dad's feet but spread across the room in seconds. The crack opened, wider and wider and shocked by what was happening, Herbert stood still. His father suddenly looked over at him, gave him a look of hate and screamed, "You did this!" As he finished the yell, the floor split open wider and Herbert's father fell into the hole. As his mother screamed, Herbert remained silent.

The earth was still moving harshly. Herbert stumbled back and forth, trying to stay still like his Mother told him. It was impossible as the floor fell in more, Herbert watched, not even letting out a scream, as his mother slipped and fell into the same crack his father did. Almost instantly, as if the monsters below the house were appeased with the offering of his mother, the earth stopped moving. Herbert, not knowing what to do, edged over the gaping hole and looked in. What he saw, what no psychologist ever believed, was Hell. The hole went down thousands of feet right into a red boiling pit of lava and a landscape of Hell itself. Herbert's mother lay on the jagged rocks, little brown monsters reminiscent of humanoid dinosaurs nibbled at her limbs. His father on the other hand was being man handled by a giant… demon. Demon was the only word Herbert could use to explain the thing, even though he saw it, looked at its eyes when it looked up to him, he could not give a clear explanation of the thing. After it looked at Herbert, it went back to his father and started to rip him to shreds.

In his cell, all these years later, he knew that the beast he had been appeasing with sacrifices, now wanted him. It wasn't happy that he stopped killing, this beast would make the earth shake open and he would swallow whoever he so desired… and Herbert knew that he was on the list. As the prison started to shake and the screams and sirens rang, Herbert remained silent, just like he did all of those years earlier. He merely backed up onto his bunk, took a seat and waited, for the floor to crack open. When it did, when he saw the floor crumble and the earth split open, he was not surprised, he was ready. As his bed started to slide into the mouth of the opening, he knew it was only a matter of time before he saw the demon from his childhood… for he had failed him and now the demon wanted revenge.

*\*Note to reader. This story is based on a real serial killer. The kills in the story actually happened and Herbert actually thought he was saving California. While the kills and the character are real, the story is purely fiction. The man just fascinated me so much I had to write about him. Lastly and most oddly, there really were NO earthquakes during his killings, though one did happen after he was put in jail.*

# GOLDEN SHOWER

The warm flow washed over him, it was wonderful, exhilarating. Being in a tropical waterfall was like heaven...then he woke up. Though he was awake, he still felt the warmth wrapping around his face, trickling into his eyes making him blink. So much so that he couldn't open them. *Salt? Why does it taste like salt?* Pungent hot salt flavor filled his mouth. Josh shot up out of his bed coughing, wiping his face trying to figure out what the hell was going on. Was there a leak in the ceiling? He couldn't think of anything else, he lived alone after all.

With his eyes stinging he was able to stumble his way to the bathroom and grab a towel. After a second he could open his eyes but his mouth still tasted horrible. Spitting and hacking he went to the sink, rinsed his mouth and washed off his face. Awake and finally thinking, Josh made his way back out of the bathroom, but quickly jumped back in fright. For there, standing on a chair next to his bed, was an old man. He was no more than four feet tall, completely naked, covered in white fuzzy body hair and bald. The man stood there with a ridiculously huge smile on his face, holding his shriveled, bent penis.

"Shit!" Josh, who was also naked, lunged for his shorts next to his bed, stumbling to put them on. He had no clue why it was the most important thing to do in the moment, but it was the first thing to come to his mind.

"Who...what? How did you get in here?" Josh yelped in panic while fumbling for the light switch. When it popped on he was even more shocked. For not only was the man's body covered in wrinkles, it was also covered in lacerations. Long slices of all different lengths were scabbed over; some still dribbled blood and puss. His eyes were the worst, they were milky white and there was hardly a shadow where the pupils once were.

The man cocked his head at Josh's voice, his face wrinkled up as if he recognized what he had said but then he let go of his penis and began clapping as if Josh had just performed an amazing act. Josh was only in his twenties and in considerably good shape, one swipe could easily take out the old man, yet he was terrified of him. Stepping back against the wall he felt around for his baseball bat, he hadn't put it back in the closet after the company softball game earlier that day. Feeling around he realized that it was on the other side of his bed, behind the old man leaning against the night stand that he had put his cell phone on.

Josh couldn't tell if the old man could see him or not. It didn't matter though; the door was close to Josh. He could easily run right out and get help. The man must have Alzheimer's or something and wandered in somehow. Though Josh couldn't figure out how since he always locked the three latches on his door. Furthermore, he lived on the third floor, with no fire escape so the windows were an impossibility to get in. That didn't matter though he just needed to go bang on his neighbor's door and get help.

As he started to shuffle his way to the door the man's milky eyes followed him. Josh didn't take his eyes off of the man as well. Four feet from the door the man started to shit himself. A line of thick chunky feces fell from the man, some catching on his legs, the rest piling on the chair. After the few first chunks, the man reached behind him cupping his hand to catch the shit. Josh was right at the door when the man flung the steaming pile right at him. It splattered on his bare shoulder, splashing a few flecks onto his face.

The smell was atrocious; Josh lurched forward and vomited immediately. Instead of heading out of the apartment he ran right back into the bathroom to wash off the shit, he couldn't get there quick enough. Inside the room he slammed the door and clicked the tiny lock shut. Then he jumped in the shower and scrubbed his face and body harshly, never taking his eyes off the door handle. Satisfied the shit was off of him, he stopped the water, dried off a bit and hesitated before going to the door. As much as he didn't want to, he knew he could only wait in there for so long. Hopefully the man had left on his own. Turning the handle on the door Josh balled up his other hand, ready to fight. He didn't see the man through the tiny slit, he opened it some more. There was still no sign of him. Slowly, carefully, he walked out and searched his tiny studio finding no sign of anyone. Turning to the door his heart skipped a beat, the door was still locked, all three of them, from the inside. The windows were also shut. When he looked more he saw that the chair was clean, no shit. However, the bed was still wet. Confused and terrified Josh saw his shorts on the bathroom floor, they were covered in shit.

Josh showered three more times that night, changed his sheets and did not go back to bed. It took him a while, but he realized it was a dream and brushed it off as a freak accident. He must have food poisoning or something. He hadn't pissed the bed since he was ten, let alone crapped himself. Had to be something he ate, yet he felt fine. That morning while eating cereal, he thought about what he ate the day before, trying to figure out what could have caused his hallucinations. *God, it was so real.*

Around the same time the next night, Josh was having the same dream about the tropical waterfall and how warm and wonderful the rushing water felt on his face. As the salty flavor seeped into his mouth, he bolted upright. This time, the stream was still coming as he sat up, he tried to block it with his hand, but the old man moved around too much, soaking every inch of Josh.

"This isn't real! I'm fucking having a dream!" He screamed out loud as the stream of piss hitting his face wore down. Grabbing the sheet he wiped his face and looked at the old man. The sight of him, the open wounds, the milky eyes, still made Josh back up, but he tried not to be scared, it was a dream after all.

"Golden shower, golden shower, golden shower!" The old man chirped in a voice that was a mix of a mad scientist and drunken leprechaun. Josh started to breathe heavy. This dream felt, sounded and even tasted too real. What the fuck was happening to him? *A dream, it had to be a dream, brought on by the stress of work.* Closing his eyes he tried to get courage to wake himself up. Pushing the man would do it, just push him off the chair and he'd wake up.

"Time to shit, Boston garage!" The voice was horrible, though not nearly as bad as the thought of being hit with the man's crap again. Jumping up, Josh ran around his bed and pushed the man just as shit was starting to dribble out his floppy ass. The man went crashing into the nightstand, shattering the lamp and knocking everything to the floor. On the ground, the man moaned in pain as he shit all over himself.

"You don't play nice. Not nice." The man cried out as if like an angry little kid. Josh put his hands on his head. *What the fuck, why am I not waking up?* Running into the bathroom he ran the water and splashed his face, repeating over and over to himself to wake up. Feeling awake, he went back into the room, it was still a mess. The sheets were wet, the lamp broken and this time, the shit was still on the floor.

The next day he called out of work and went to the doctors for help. He didn't tell them all the details, not wanting to be labeled as crazy, but he got a prescription for a sleeping pill. At least he'd get some sleep this time. With a fresh set of sheets and two sleeping pills in his stomach, Josh drifted off, praying he would have a peaceful night. That night he had no dreams, none at all, though he did wake up in a panic, gasping for air. Drowsy from the drugs, Josh had to roll to his side and empty his mouth and spit several times before he could breathe. Before he could even suck in enough air, the smell and taste hit him. Immediately he started to vomit. In the background he could hear the old man laughing. Stopping three times to puke on the way to the bathroom, Josh finally made it to the shower. Letting the water spray his face and into his mouth he did his best to not throw up again, but as he watched the chunk of shit clog up the drain, he had to puke at the thought that the old man had shit in his mouth as he slept.

A twenty minute shower and a half of bottle of Listerine later, Josh was ready to face the man, *if* he was still there. Filled with rage he swung open the bathroom door to see the old man lying on the bed, stroking his tiny penis. The man laughed at the sight of Josh.

"You are fucking dead old man!" Grabbing the bat that he now kept in the bathroom, he raced towards the man. With one hard downward swing, the bat made contact with the man's groin and the hand that was stroking it. The scream was horrendous, but it didn't stop Josh from taking another one, this time to the man's chest. The cracking sound churned his stomach, but he wasn't going to stop. The man wasn't real, so it didn't matter, all he had to do was kill him and the man would disappear and be out of his mind forever. Raising the bat for the third time, the man screamed.

"Wait!" Not knowing why, Josh obeyed, but kept his bat ready.

"What, what, what!?" He screamed like a mad man himself. The old man touched his chest in pain, but then smiled.

"Golden shower..." The old man eked out. Josh snapped. He didn't want to hit the man again; he wanted to do the same thing to him, to show him what it was like. Throwing the bat aside he jumped up on the bed, pulled his dick out of his shorts and aimed right at the man's face.

"I'll give you a golden shower you sick bastard." As he started to piss on the man's face, Josh realized how insane he was being right now; he was pissing on an imaginary man's face. He started to laugh hysterically. When he saw that the old man seemed to enjoy the piss on his face, so much so that he was opening his mouth greedily accepting the piss, he laughed even harder.

When the stream was done, Josh jumped off the bed still laughing, wondering when the old bastard would disappear and he'd wake up. Watching the man lick his lips a few times, Josh started to get annoyed.

"Leave! Disappear, go the fuck away!" Picking up the bat he started to swing it at anything and everything. He hit the bed post, smacked the door frame and broke the new lamp he bought that afternoon... yet the man didn't disappear. The old man just sat there, moaning holding his ribs and petting his crooked hard on. Not being able to take it anymore, he finally swung the bat down on the man's head. It caved in like a hard-boiled egg being hit with a fork. The crushed face oozed blood, but the man did not disappear. Still having frustration in him, Josh swung the bat at the wall next to the refrigerator, the wall crumbled in, just like the man's face. *What the fuck?* Leaning down to investigate, he pushed the wall in, it moved with ease. *A hidden door?* Crawling through the opening, he found himself inside of the next apartment... the old man's apartment.

"I'm... I'm not crazy!" Josh screamed and laughed to himself. *But wait a minute... If I'm not crazy, then everything that happened was real. A man shit in my mouth and... and... I killed someone.*

# DON'T MESS WITH THE DEAD

Rich spent almost an hour a day working on it, and yet, he still could never get it how she would want it. No matter how much he arranged stuff, clipped the grass, dusted and polished the stone, he just knew she wouldn't be happy with how it looked. Not that she would complain… she never did. In life she would just smile at something he did, then wait for him to leave and she would fix it the way she wanted. That's why he never felt like he could ever get her grave the way she would like it, because for that to happen, she would have to do it herself.

Sitting back on his feet the wiped he dirt off his gloves. The picture of Donna sat frozen in Lucite, embedded in the smooth black marble, staring out at him. Her beautiful smile was a constant reminder that he had lost her; that she was gone. Checking his watch he realized he had once again been there for over an hour, well over an hour. Looking down at the solar powered lights arranged on the sides, the fresh flowers he planted (the third variety this week, none of the ones he planted seemed good enough) and the knick knacks he placed and moved a dozen times, he sighed and stood up.

"Tomorrow my love, tomorrow I will get it right." It was the same thing he said every night before getting up, packing his tools into his pick up and heading home to eat and then drink himself to sleep.

99

At work, Rich would talk to no one. Not that he talked much before. He simply loaded the trucks with the pallets on the order slip, took his breaks and went to the graveyard right after work. On the weekends he found himself spending half the day sitting next to a cold marble slab trying not to think about what his wife's body looked like under all that dirt. Reading was not something he enjoyed; Donna on the other hand loved trashy romance novels. So, on days when he got fed up with fussing with the placement of decorative rocks and mulch, he sat and read out loud to her.

The graveyard was a good hundred yards in each direction with the older stones towards the front, by the main road. Donna's grave was in the back, with the rest of the new ones. It was the busier area of graveyard. At times when he sat there a dozen people would go by, though most of them just going for a walk. The up and down rows made it a favorite walking ground in the small town. He always ignored anyone who came close, though most would skip his row to be polite anyway. The few who walked by would give him a pathetic smile to show they were sorry.

Work, visit Donna, sleep; day in and day out for those first few months after Donna died, that was how his life went. There was nothing else. He no longer read the newspaper, it disgusted him and television was only on at the house to keep the silence from making him go insane. As the days went by, the only things that seemed to change were the decorations he used to lighten up her grave. That was the way things went, the way he thought they would go until he too died, which couldn't be soon enough for him.

Everything changed one Saturday morning. He got up, got dressed and made sure the truck was loaded with what he needed for the day. Being that it was the weekend, he put a folding chair, a cooler filled with food and drinks, a new romance novel and several new solar lights he was going to swap out the old ones with, into the truck. The drive was only two miles and took him about five minutes. He drove in silence, breathing steadily to keep himself calm. It was a technique a therapist taught him during the one session he went to. Breathe deep and slow to keep yourself from exploding. Something he felt like he was always on the edge of. When he arrived at the graveyard his breathing sped up a bit as he saw police cars blocking the entrance and exit.

When he tried to pull in the cop signaled for him to keep driving. Frustrated, he pulled into the church parking lot across the street and jumped out, eager to find out why he couldn't go see his wife. He darted across the street causing a few cars to honk and the cops to give him a dirty look. Trying to breathe deep to not get mad, he walked up to the cop that had waved him on.

"What's going on? I want to visit my wife." He refused to follow *wife* with *grave*. The cop for some reason wouldn't look at him in the face when he answered.

"Eh, some kids vandalized the graveyard." There was flashing in front of his eyes as he watched the cop act nonchalant. Vandals? Donna, was she all right?

"What did they do? Is everything all right? I have to see my wife, make sure they didn't harm her." The cop looked at the ground and kicked a pebble.

"They kicked over some of the old headstones and spray painted some others. A real mess." Rich started to walk hurriedly past the officer.

"Hey, sir! You have to wait. They are taking pictures of the mess, they'll be done in a bit. Uh, someone will contact you if there was harm done to one of your loved one's graves." The officer said as if reading off a note card. Rich ignored him and raced up the drive not caring if the officer followed or not. Less than ten yards in he stopped as if he hit a brick wall. The entire graveyard, from the 1700's graves in the front to the new ones in the back was violated. Dozens kicked over, toilet paper strewn about, orange and red graffiti sprayed haphazardly over graves and trees alike.

Donna's grave was in the far back, a good fifty or more yards from where Rich stood. He was terrified to see if Donna was all right. Instead of racing back, he glanced around to see his odds. It seemed that about half the graves got away scot-free while the others were damaged. As he took painfully slow steps, he was oblivious to the dozens of cops.; the caretakers eager to clean up; the priests praying in a small group by the angel memorial, which now had spray-painted clown makeup on its face, in the center; the news crews pulling up, doing their best to get shots. No one and nothing mattered, except for Donna. As he walked to the back he took deep breaths, knowing that if something was wrong with her grave, this breathing technique was useless.

Thirty yards away, he fell to his knees. His fists clenched and a low growl came out from his chest, a sound he never heard himself make. He doubled over, his fists punching the ground. Lifting his head he took one more look at the giant neon orange letters sprayed on Donna's grave, *BITCH,* with a big arrow pointing to her picture. Seeing it again, he blacked out.

After refusing treatment, Rich knelt in front of Donna's grave. With his thumb he tried to wipe of some of the paint. It did nothing but smudge a bit. Placing both hands on top of the grave he dropped his head and mumbled to Donna.

"I'm so sorry baby, I'm so sorry." He fought back tears, as he knew dozens of people were still around.

"I'll get this cleaned up, get you a new stone if I have to. And I will find who did this. I will find them and I will make them pay." He hadn't even thought about the words as they came out. They merely just fell out of his mouth without thinking. Hearing himself say them, he knew it was exactly what he had to do. Clean her headstone first, then, prepare to get revenge and protect the graveyard from this happening again.

After a quick run to the store and an hour of scrubbing he realized the fowl letters would not come off easily. The color did slowly disappear as his fingers started to tear from scratching the steel wool back and forth. Taking a break, wiping the sweat from his forehead he saw that the though the color was disappearing, the scratches he was making would be there forever.

"I'll get you a new stone my love, a better one. I'll go right now." Cleaning up his mess he looked at the stone to make sure the word and arrow was unreadable. Satisfied, but still fuming, he jumped in his truck and headed for the same place he bought this headstone. It was in town and only a few minute's drive (conveniently located next to a funeral home). The place was small and discreet with just a few slabs of fancy marble outside of it that showed it was a store of some sort.

Once inside he was instantly greeted by a small man, not the man he remembered from his first trip here over a year ago. The man greeted him solemnly, carefully assessing the situation. Rich knew what he wanted, so he dispatched with all the pleasantries.

"Look, my wife's stone was desecrated, I need a new one. I want it in by the weekend, I don't care at what cost." Rich knew that normally it took several if not six or more months to get a stone put in, ridiculous by all means. There was no way he could let Donna suffer that long without a stone. The small man made a comment on how he heard about the graveyard, how it was "a shame', "such a shame". Rich didn't even bother looking at the man; instead he kept his eyes on the smooth black stone on display behind the counter. The new stone would cost him his entire savings probably, especially with the rush order put on it, but it didn't matter anymore. Nothing mattered.

Filling out the forms, being careful to make sure all the letters were spelled out right and clear, Rich got a glimpse of the short man talking to two more customers who had come in. The man had that same solemn tone he used on Rich, but Rich knew the man was probably thrilled with all the extra business the vandalism was bringing him. Hell, they would make more off of Donna's grave then he made in almost a year alone. It was sick making money off of the dead like that. He had to push the ideas out of his head to finish the form and write the check. At first the man had said there was no way he could get it to him by the weekend, a week maybe, but with a thousand dollar tip the man said he would pull some strings. Before he left, the man, who he now noticed looked like a mole, only with more hair, having tiny puffs coming out his nose and ears, checked the form and pocketed his thousand dollar check. Rich merely scoffed at him and mumbled how the grave better be on time.

The rest of the week he spent getting supplies of all kinds. Rope, zip ties, knifes (half a dozen all different sizes), spray paint, toilet paper, food, cooler, halogen lamps, camping supplies and fresh flowers for the new grave. Friday morning he arrived just as the crane was pulling out the old headstone. Part of him wanted to keep it, to put it in the backyard (even though he hasn't entered the yard since she died). The other part of him wanted it to be destroyed, demolished, shattered into a thousand pieces, so that no one would ever see the fowl word that was once splashed across it. As it was loaded on the back of the flatbed truck he watched it drive away. Suddenly he raced after the truck, which stopped only after a few yards of him chasing it. When it came to a stop he jumped up on the back of the truck bed, pulled out his new knife and worked at removing Donna's picture. The driver first jumped out annoyed, but Rich gave him a look that was returned with just a nod that said the man understood.

With his fingers caressing the cold Lucite picture of his dead wife he paced back and forth. Every time he looked at the patch of dirt where the headstone should be he winced. It was like someone had taken away Donna's name, her identity; it was as if she didn't exist without that headstone. Checking his watch, the watch she gave him on their tenth anniversary, he started to get worried. It was getting late; almost four in the afternoon. The gravestone was supposed to be in by three, the grounds crew would be leaving soon. Flipping open his cell he dialed the number he remembered by heart just in case it didn't show. Within a few seconds he heard the short man's voice on the phone assuring him that it was on the way, in fact he would meet him there to assure it showed up.

Within twenty minutes a sleek black Jaguar pulled in, followed by a different flatbed truck. Rich could feel himself relax a bit. The short man got out of his car and offered a hand to Rich, which he took, all the while he keeping his eyes on the lump under the burlap cover on the flatbed. Before the driver was even out of the truck, Rich was climbing up the back and undoing the straps. He heard the driver yell at him, then the small man hushing him saying it was alright. Uncovering the gravestone he couldn't help but smile, it was even better than the last one. Same color and stone, but bigger,

105

fancier etchings and the picture of Donna was twice the size of the last one.

"It has the sealant on it, just like you asked! Someone sprays this one, it will wipe right off." Rich heard over his shoulder. He acknowledged it with a nod.

For the next hour Rich hovered over the three workers who set the stone in place. The small man who sold him the grave, (who he finally learned was named James even though he must have heard it several times before) tried in vain several times to pull him away with conversation and offers of coffee, Rich ignored him.

"Think they will beef up the security in the graveyard now? I mean really, there is none; all they do is close the gates at night. Some days that is, half the time it's left wide open. No cameras, no lights, nothing." James the grave salesman said over Rich's shoulder.

"I doubt they will, but I'll be doing something about it." Rich mumbled more to himself than to James. Unfortunately, it peaked the man's interest.

"Really? You going to invest some money into this place?" The man asked him incredulously.

"Something like that." James tried several times to find out more about what he meant, but Rich refused to give up any more information.

When the gravestone was set in and polished off, Rich couldn't help but smile. It was beautiful, Donna would have loved it. Rich could hear the truck drive off behind him as he kept looking for fingerprints to wipe off. He had completely forgotten about James when he heard a small cough behind him. He turned and gave the man the best, *what are you still doing here* look.

"Well, I hope you are happy sir. I guess I'll take off now." Rich stood up and offered his hand, not even sure why the man came down in the first place.

"Very happy, thank you." With a firm handshake the man took off in his expensive car and Rich finished making the grave looked as best as he could.

The first night he didn't go all out. He was tired and needed his rest for the next day. He parked his car across the street at the church and took two knifes, the lantern, some food and a sleeping bag. He had been camping many times so he was used to the hard and uncomfortable ground. Sleep came easy; he didn't even wake up once, not until the morning sun got in his eyes forcing him to get up.

Grumbling a hello to his wife's headstone he stood up and stretched out. He was a bit wet from the morning dew, but he would dry soon. Taking a quick look he made sure no one was around as he took a leak into a large bottle, apologizing to Donna while doing so. Next he ate a granola bar for breakfast while waiting for the sun to burn off the morning dew. As he let the sun beat down on him he took a walk to look at the perimeter of the graveyard. There were only three ways to get in. Two were on Main Street: one was the entrance, a single lane old road that led its way in, and the other the exit, the same thing that headed out. There was nothing stopping people from coming in either of them. At night the gate was shut by a weak latch, which didn't matter anyway as anyone but an invalid could step over or through the giant gaps in it. The third entrance was a bit wider road in the way back that led off to Elm Street. This was only added a decade ago, as expansions were needed. Fortunately that entrance had a sturdy gate, though it was hardly closed. The rest of the cemetery was encased in an old wrought iron fence or stretches of woods. Standing next to the fence, Rich figured it was about teen feet high. Gripping it he tried to climb up it. Now he wasn't a teen, but he figured even they wouldn't risk climbing over it, with the

107

giant fleur-de-lis spikes on top of each poll. Even if they did, he had a plan for that.

Throughout the day people came and went. Rich forced smiles and polite waves as he went about his tasks, which included a lot of complicated work. To get away with it he pretended to be a grounds man. No one asked him questions or tried to stop him. He was comfortable doing this because he knew the real groundskeeper only worked on the weekdays. By the time the sun was setting he had everything he needed in place. He took stock of what he had done, checked everything and was pleased that it was all in working order. He washed up using a towel and one of the hoses for the flowers before eating a meal consisting of a cold can of beans and water.

"I don't know if they are stupid enough to try again, but I hope to hell they do though Donna, I hope they do." He grumbled as he finished off the can.

As the sun set that night, he once again set up his sleeping bag; although this time he didn't plan on staying in it for long. He would nap, but every hour on the hour, he would get up and make his rounds. The full perimeter would be traced and he would check every entrance to make sure no one came in. If they did, he would take care of them, each and every one of them. He'd find out which one wrote on Donna's grave and he'd make that one pay the most. With thoughts of getting revenge bouncing around in his head, he couldn't fall asleep, so he stayed awake until the first check. Unfortunately, all was clear.

The second and third shifts were the same, only this time he managed to get some sleep in between them. It was three in the morning when he had his first jolt of excitement. Right before his next check was to start; his alarm had gone off (he used his cell on vibrate in his shirt pocket to make no noise). As he sleepily rubbed his eyes, wondering if what he was doing was stupid, he heard a noise. It was a small stick cracking noise coming from the front of the graveyard. He bolted up, looked off in the distance, but couldn't see a thing in the dark. Climbing out of his bag, he started his sneaky ascent to the front by ducking behind grave after grave.

Near the front, he still couldn't see much, but then, Rich heard the low rumble of a burp a few feet in front of him. With a knife in his hand, he took a peek over the old crumbling stone. In the shadows he could see the back of a man with a denim coat on wavering back and forth with his hands in front of him. Deciding not to wait to take the opportunity, Rich sprung into action and ran at the figure. He reached him in a second, wrapped his arms around his front and put the knife to his neck.

"Move an inch you fuck and I'll make sure you end up under the ground with the graves you destroyed." Rich whispered, having waited to say that line, rehearsing it in his head over and over again.

"Jesus Christ! I'm pissing all over myself, what the fuck is going on?" Rich took a few deep breaths, looked around, then tried to see the face of the man. He was unshaven; a man in his forties, maybe older.

"I'm just taking a piss man, you can take my wallet if you want, just don't, damn it, don't stab me." The man squealed through a raspy breath. Rich pushed him away, letting him go, but kept his knife aimed at him. Looking around he noticed he was only a few feet in the cemetery, near the entrance. He looked back to the man who had put his arms up.

"What are you doing in here?" Rich demanded.

"Just taking a piss, I know it's wrong, but, I couldn't hold it till I got home and I have another four streets to walk and if I went out there and someone saw me I could get a ticket and I can't afford that, I just lost

109

my car and…" The man rambled on and on till Rich cut him off. Easing up, Rich let the knife lower a bit.

"Get out of here." He said almost embarrassed. Trudging back to his campsite he felt the adrenaline ease away. His chest ached a bit and he wondered if his heart would hold out through all of this. The rest of the night was silent, too silent.

Three uneventful nights went by. Rich left from time to time to stock up on supplies and to disappear while the groundskeepers came in on the weekends. He was using his vacation time and called in on Sunday to say he was going to be out the next week as well. Stopping at the police station during one of his stock up runs, he asked for the detective on the case and was given the run around. After waiting for a few hours an officer told him there were no leads in the case, but they were still looking. Hearing this news just made Rich all the more anxious to get the bastards who hurt his wife.

Sunday, on his way back to the graveyard, he picked up a newspaper. As he started to drive, he glanced over at the paper on the seat next to him and almost crashed. There on the front page he saw in huge letters; *Another Grave Vandalism*. Pulling over he read the story three times. It was the same bastards that hit his place, at least the police think, because of the same sort of paint used. Rich balled up the paper, threw it at the floor and screamed in the cab of his truck. Part of him was angry for not staking out other graveyards, but mostly he was furious that others were going to feel the way he felt.

Back at the graveyard, Rich parked back in front of Donna's stone. He told her about the other graveyard, about how he had to get these kids before they struck again, but what more could he do? If he left this graveyard, he was leaving her vulnerable. Even if he did take that risk, what graveyard would he choose to watch?

"Hell, if they already hit here, they probably wouldn't come back. Though I can't take that chance, leaving you vulnerable to anyone. I mean what would I do? Pick a random graveyard out of the hundreds to sit in and hope it's the one they pick?" He took a big breath as he could hear Donna's voice in his head, telling him to calm down. He slowed his pace and finally sat down.

"I'll stay with you. Keep you safe. I guess that is all I can do." He pulled his knees up to his chest, held them there and stared at his wife's picture. He didn't want to cry, he didn't want to be weak, but he couldn't help it. The sun set as the tears fell down his cheeks and onto his shirt.

Once again he set up camp and settled in for the night. Though this night he decided not to do rounds. He was at Donna's grave, if anyone came near, he'd wake up and that was all that mattered. Washed of emotions he slept soundly that night...until a low metal clicking noise followed by a hiss woke him. As his eyes snapped open, he lay still, trying to figure out if it was a dream, a snake, or them. As his sleep cleared, he listened harder to the noise, there was no doubt, it was a spray can. *They were back.* His heart started to race as he quietly checked his knives. They were all there; he just had to get up silently so he wouldn't scare them off.

Slipping out of his bag was the hardest part. He was afraid unzipping it would make too much noise. It took a lot of sliding and squirming but he made it out the end of the bag without using the zipper. Finally able to crawl, he took position behind a large headstone near Donna's and peaked out. About twenty rows away he could see a shadowy figure moving about, the sound of the can shaking and spraying was indisputable. These were the vandals. Figuring there was more than one, Rich scrambled back to his bag and slipped out his infrared

111

binoculars. Back behind the stone he quickly scanned the entire cemetery. There were two more vandals to the far right. *Bingo, this was it.* He could pick the one by himself him off first, then head to the other two, hopefully they will separate for a few minutes.

The journey to the front of the graveyard was quick and quiet; his footsteps were silent on the grass. A few feet behind the vandal, who was now kicking over headstones, Rich felt his body start to go weak, he was terrified. It wasn't until that moment that he realized that he had never hurt anyone, let alone been in a fight. He just hoped seeing all those action movies over the years would translate to his actions. As the man kicked over another stone he stopped and took a break, breathing hard. Without thinking, without counting to three in his head, Rich raced forward, dove on the man's back, covered the small man's mouth and quickly, without even thinking about it, stuck the knife into his ribs. The two fell into a crumbled pile on the ground. Rich could feel the man's wet hot scream on his fingers covering the man's mouth. His other hand felt the warmth of blood flooding over them.

Lying there, using his weight to keep the man down, Rich didn't move. He had stabbed him, and unless he got help quickly, the man would die. *Why had he stabbed him? He meant to scare them, teach them a lesson, but not kill them.* He had to get help, but the sirens from the fire station only a half-mile away would scare them off, the others would get away. With a deep breath, Rich closed his eyes, twisted the knife, pulled it out and plunged it back in several more times until the hot air on his hands stopped coming out. When the breathing stopped, he waited even a few minutes longer. As he got up he looked down at the back of the man he just killed. The body wore black jeans and a black sweater. Rich couldn't resist rolling the body over to see the face of the man he just murdered. As the body flopped lifelessly onto its back, he saw that it was not a man and in fact... a teenager, no more than fifteen at most. *What did he expect, of course it was teenagers.* He started to feel dizzy for a moment, but the sound of two other spray cans snapped him out of it. They were close to his wife's grave, too close.

Trying not to make a sound, Rich walked toward the other two; their backs were to him as they were both crouching down spraying graves. He knew in that instant, he could kill them both... and not feel guilty. The first one may have been hard, but like they say, the first is always the hardest. Wiping the blood off on his pants, he made sure the knife was dry so it wouldn't slip from his hand as he approached what he assumed was another stupid teen. As Rich took the last step, a twig snapped under his foot. The kid turned to him with wide eyes and yelped like a scared dog.

"Jesus! You scared the shit out of me man, I, we were just..." The kid's eyes saw the knife in Rich's hand and realized there was more going on than just being caught, at least Rich hoped he realized that. He swung the knife straight ahead, one sharp jab that missed. The kid was young and fit and able to move out of the way. The blade hit the headstone with a tiny spark. The kid crawled away and tried to get up, giving Rich the extra second he needed to adjust his attack. Just as the kid was in a running stance Rich was able to sink the knife into the kid's calf muscle. The scream was loud and piercing, it made Rich smile. He pulled the knife towards him, down the kid's calf. It caught a few times, there was snapping and scraping noises, but he was able to pull it down a good six inches. The kid was going nowhere.

Satisfied that he had time to go after the other kid, Rich stood up to see where he had run off too. The dark

113

shadow was heading towards the back of the graveyard much slower than Rich expected for a teen to run. As he went to run after him, the kid with the split calf wouldn't stop screaming. Knowing he had a bit of time, Rich crouched down and grabbed the kid's face. He tried to get away from Rich's grip but that just forced Rich to squeeze harder.

"You don't mess with the dead kid." Rich enjoyed seeing the horror in the teen's eyes as he said the words in his best Dirty Harry voice. Then with one swift swipe, Rich slashed the knife across the kid's throat. He could feel a warm splash of blood hit his own face, but ignored it and the gurgling boy as he got up to go after the last one.

Feeling alive for the first time since Donna died, Rich sprinted to the back of the cemetery, anxious to get his hands on the last one. Being only one left, he thought about how he could take his time with this one; make him pay for what he did to Donna. Surprisingly, it didn't take long for Rich to catch up. In fact, he stopped a good twenty yards behind the figure to watch as the kid fell right into his trap. Rich strolled, holding back a laugh, as the figure reached for the old iron fence, took a step and jumped, grabbing it with both hands to climb over. Rich couldn't help but let out a hoot as a brilliant blue and yellow spark shot up and the figure flew back a few feet, hitting his back hard on a marble gravestone. It was definitely worth the two hundred bucks he spent on buying four car batteries and hooking them up to the fence with jumper cables.

The whimpering figure was on his stomach when he reached him. Rich's mind started to wander about what exactly he should do with him. How should he make him pay for his sins? With one startling hard kick to the ribs the boy, dressed in black, flipped over. Rich's smile disappeared as he saw the face, the boiling blood lust in his mind sputtered with confusion as it was not a boy at all, but a man, a man he knew. He had to blink a few times before he connected the face to *who* it was, even when he realized who it was, it took him a few more seconds to figure out why James, the man who sold him Donna's headstone, twice, was here.

"Wait, wait, don't hurt me, I can explain." James cried out, holding his ribs with burnt hands.

"There is no explanation that will save your life, none at all." Rich barked out feeling the blood lust rise to new heights.

"You don't understand, my business, it's been in my family for years. It was going to close, we weren't making enough money. I had to, I had to do something. That's why I started to vandalize the graves." James coughed a bit as Rich just stood there stiff as a board, his mind blank.

"I figured if we did it, then people would come and buy new stones and I could make enough money to save the business. It was stupid, but I was desperate. I'm so sorry, I never meant anything by it. You understand don't you? I have a family, I had to provide for them." Rich cracked his neck, shrugged his shoulders. He could feel the rage building in his body, but he held it back, wanted to let the man keep spilling his guts… not that it mattered.

"What about the kids? They your boys?" Rich asked in a whispered tone.

"No, no, just some kids I found skateboarding one night. I paid them a hundred bucks each to help out. What did you to do them anyway? I heard screaming, you let them go, I hope?" Rich laughed a bit as he looked back towards the shadowy bodies that lie on the ground in the distance.

115

"Let's just say I just made you two potential sales." The man started to cry, he put his hands over his face and sat up.

"I'll do whatever you want, please sir. I'll turn myself in, I'll pay to have every single grave fixed. I'll donate money to the graveyards, I'll do community service, I'll get your wife a bigger stone, free of course. Whatever you want, I'll do it." Hearing the man mention his wife was the last straw, he had played enough games.

"Stand up." Rich demanded and the man obliged. He made James turn around and walk towards the front of the graveyard. First he wanted to show him the bodies of the kids, the ones he was responsible for getting killed, then, then he would get his revenge. The last words the salesman every heard were, "What type of headstone are you going to get James? I hope you get the sealant on it, because it would be a shame if someone ever defaced it."

The next day, Rich was looking online for information about exhuming Donna's body and having it cremated. If he did that, then he could always have her with him and no one could mess with her. As he read about the laws of exhuming, he heard the television in the den say there was breaking news. Getting up he was curious as to what it was.

Standing in the doorway with a small smile, he watched the news report of the *massacre in the graveyard*, as they called it. So far there weren't many details, only that three bodies had been found, two propped against graves, the third hanging from a tree. Reports of eyewitnesses said that the bodies all had orange spray painted words on their shirts. One body had one word, the other two had two words each. When read in order, the words said...
*Don't Mess With The Dead.*

# GOD'S WHORES
## (Inspired by True Events)


Until the age of fourteen I thought everyone's parents slept with them. Now I don't mean *mommy I'm scared, can I sleep in your bed*, type of sleeping. I mean it in the sexual way. I know to you, this thought is horrific, but if you are raised with doing that from as long as you can remember, it's normal. That's why when I was told it was *wrong*, I did not understand why. To me it was as normal as taking a shower every day. It was a routine, something you did. You hopped into bed with mom, dad and your brother and all of you touched and played with each other until mom and dad were tired. I enjoyed it too, as sick as it sounds, as much as counselors tell me I didn't, that it was abuse, I liked it. It was our family time and I got physical pleasure out of it. If I was a boy like Jim, my brother, maybe I would have enjoyed it even more, but I still liked it nonetheless.

You see, I was raised in a cult, at least that is what outsiders called it, we viewed it as a religious group. The group was called the Children of The Lord. Now I won't bore you with a detailed sermon about our beliefs or practices. I'm not here to convert you, especially since the group has officially been "disbanded". However, I do need to give you a quick rundown so you understand my story. It was founded in the sixties by a man named Arnold Simon. God spoke to him and told him that physical love was the way into heaven. He started to preach, people started to follow and by the seventies we had over ten thousand members worldwide. We were a peaceful group that lived together in communes and practiced free love. Money was made through farming and handmade goods that were sold at markets. The group would still be thriving if it weren't for the child molestation investigations.

In the late nineties a dozen arrests were made and the group was forced to disband. Children, like myself, were placed into foster care. I was sixteen at the time so I didn't have to live with strangers for too long, but let me tell you, having "family time" with my real parents was much better than living with a father figure who beat me if I did anything wrong. Now, I hope you have a decent understanding of the group, if you don't, look us up and learn more about what the specific beliefs were, I don't have time to go over them here.

Let's get to the point of this talk. In Children there were two methods of recruiting new members, through traditional literature and lectures and a method developed in the eighties that got the recruiters nicknamed, "God's Whores". My mother was one of them. The best looking women of our group would be sent out at night to go to clubs. They would flirt and seduce men. They would take them home and have crazy, wild sex that would blow their minds. Then in the morning they would wake them up with breakfast in bed and a blow-job. The men would think they were in heaven and that was exactly the point. After the B&BJ (the slang they used for the method) they would pull out a brochure on our religion, which was filled with many pictures of graphic sex. They would then (while caressing them more) tell them about how if they joined, they could have sex with hundreds of different women a week, that there were orgies and you didn't have to work a normal job. Pretty much every single guy who hated his job and only got laid once a month joined.

Like I said, my mother was one of these GW's. During my childhood she was home most nights, but then, as I got older she started to go out three to four times a week to recruit. She would often come back with a new man that we were all expected to offer ourselves to. Again, this was something that was normal to me. I never once left the commune and we were hardly allowed to watch television or movies. So to me, the outside world, and with that, all its morals, hardly existed. Offering my body to a complete stranger and knowing how to please a full-grown man better than most grown women at the age of eleven was normal. It was my purpose in the world. It was what I was good at and trained to do. In fact, my father said I was so good that men in our commune had to schedule time with me because so many wanted my services. By the time I was thirteen, there were days when I would be with almost twenty-five men.

In a way you can look at it like your job. You go to work for eight hours a day, doing something you learned to do. You get good at it, some days you hate it, some days you love it, but what it comes down to, it is what you do. Sex, was what I did. It was all I knew from age five and up. We were home schooled, but very little, only things that were essential, mostly basic math, reading and writing. I knew nothing of the history of the world or of science. When I went into foster care they put me into tenth grade according to my age. I knew nothing; I was so behind it was sad. That, and I despised the formal setting of a classroom and structured time of having to be in a place. On our commune, we were free to go as we please (of course we had to please those who asked, when they asked). I was kicked out of five schools in three years, all

119

for having sex with fellow students and a few teachers. As much as they told me, I didn't know what I was doing was wrong, I thought they were wrong.

People hated me, called me a slut and a whore. It took a while for me to realize that it was hatred. For *whore*, where I came from, was an honorable position that only the most beautiful and talented could obtain. I hated the world, I missed my parents and I wanted to be back in the commune. The counselor I was forced to see four times a week tried to tell me that I was "conditioned", that this was the real world and the way things should be. I told them I didn't care, that our world was better. I also got pushed around from foster parents to foster parents. Mostly they got rid of me for, you guessed it, having sex. I slept with three of my foster dads and twelve of my foster brothers.

Thankfully I turned eighteen and was allowed to go my own way. I went and found our old commune out in the New England woods, but it was now a strip mall. I didn't know what to do after that. I had no money, only two pairs of clothes and nowhere to go. I started to prostitute myself, standing on street corners, finding men in grocery stores and talking them into spending their money on me instead of food for their families. Slowly but surely I made some money, hiding it carefully while living in the woods and showering in the sink of a park bathroom. I stole cosmetics to make myself look clean, fresh and sexy and slept my way to ten thousand dollars within a year. I used that money as a down payment on an apartment and furnishings.

Though I enjoyed sex my whole life, the sex I was having now was different. The men weren't having sex with me for God, they weren't loving me, they weren't gentle like all my fellow believers were growing up. This sex was animalistic, dirty, wrong, secretive and often abusive. It was during these times, when men told me I was the best they ever had, that I realized that our religion was right, that we *were* doing things the way God wanted them to be. Our society was happy, carefree and loving. This so called "real world" was dark, mean and worthless. When I came to this point of realization, I knew I had to start our society again. I just had to make some more money first.

I was with a new client, he seemed alright at first, but things changed quickly when he started to screw me. His thrusts were harder than normal men; his grip was tight on my hip. Then, as he was behind me, he reached down and started choking me. His grip was so hard that I knew I wouldn't last more than a minute, not only was I not getting air, he was crushing my throat. With the little energy I had I reached for my emergency knife I had stashed under the cushion. I got it without a problem (I always left the blade under the cushion and the handle sticking out for easy grabbing), swung my arm back, and hit him in the face. He instantly let go and fell out of me onto the bed. Getting up, I readied the knife, hoping he would grab his clothing and run. It was then I heard the voice in my ear, it was only in my right ear, which made me know it was real, if I was hallucinating it would be in my head, this, this was in my ear as if someone whispered it. *He is unholy, vile and evil, rid the earth of this plague.* There was no doubt in the world to me, the voice was that of… God. The feeling his voice gave me was better than any orgasm I ever had. Without a second thought I leapt over the bed and stabbed the man, who was frantically trying to put on his pants, in the back. He screamed, I pulled the knife out and stabbed him the neck to silence him.

As the man lay on my floor, staining it with his blood as he slowly died, I heard the voice again. *You are the one I choose to bring the Children of the Lord back to its glory.*

*This time, to survive and make this world heaven on earth, we must rid it of those who are not pure enough to understand our mission. Those like that man there. Become like your mother, recruit and start a new home, become a whore for me and dispatch of those who do not want to or do not understand enough to participate. Do whatever you have to do to succeed. I am counting on you.* When the voice disappeared I screamed out a million questions, how do I get rid of a body that is twice my size, how do I get money to buy land for a commune, how to I get women to join? Nothing was answered and I knew he was challenging me to discover these answers on my own.

Over the next five months I killed fifteen clients, disposed of their bodies by cutting them up in my bathtub and dumping their parts piece by piece in the local river. I was never worried about getting caught, I had God on my side. Each time I killed one, I took their cash and went to ATMs and took out what I could (I started asking for pin numbers when I had the knife to their throats). I was getting a small stockpile of money and when I had enough, I bought a car and expanded my work to other cities to lessen suspicion. When I killed men outside of my apartment, I just dumped the bodies wherever I was. After a month I had sixty thousand dollars in cash. I packed up all my belongings and drove here to Nevada where I could buy land for a thousand dollars an acre. I bought fifty acres, a small camper and drank a full bottle of wine as I sat on what was going to be the new commune. It was then time to find members.

I got two weak men to join rather easily, though after that it was hard. No one wanted to share a woman with three guys and live in a tiny trailer. It was hard, but I got a few more women to join, bought a few more trailers and kept recruiting. We have been growing in the past year, but we need a lot more money, a lot more to grow to the numbers God desires. So that has brought us up to speed and I hope that explains why I am here tonight. I did my research; I found out that you are worth over twenty million dollars and that you have a fondness for women. I knew it would be easy to seduce you, easy to get you tied up and gag you like I have you now. The hard part was getting you to listen; it's why I have you like this. Rumor has it that your bodyguards kick women out by eight in the morning. That gives you less than an hour to make a decision. Though I am the chosen one, the Messiah if you will, I still need someone else to sit on the throne with me. I am making this offer to you once, the offer to be the king of our commune, you and I will rule it and eventually the world. I did the math, if you sell off your assets you will have over forty-million cash. All we need to start the commune is thirty-million. Together we can design and build it, then with your power we recruit more and more people until eventually, we rule the world.

What is in it for you? I'm sure you are asking yourself that. Well two things. One, you get to live. If you say no I will slit your throat and slip out of this building before anyone can find out that you are dead. I think that is a pretty convincing one. Secondly, you will rule evenly with me. We would go down in history as the new Adam and Eve, only, we'd rule the world instead of being punished. With your obsession with power, I know that must appeal to you. Lastly, you get to have unlimited sex. You might think you can now, since you are rich, but in our commune you can have thousands of women at one time, sex with any age, men, women, orgies, anything you want twenty-four hours a day and all without having to hide it from anyone. Think about it, power, sex and a place in history. It's either that or…death. As for killing the non-believers, don't worry, I'll handle that along with a special team. You'll never have to get your hands dirty.

By the way, if you think that all you have to do is say yes and that I'll leave and you'll be fine with your body guards, you are wrong. If you try to trick me, I have a backup plan that would actually screw you more than sex. You see, I have already squeezed the semen out of the condom you threw away. I put some inside of me. I also scratched up my back and arms with your nails when you were unconscious. I will have one of my boys rough me up a bit more, then I'll go right to the police and scream rape. I might not win in court, but it will make your life miserable for a while. Then after that, I'll still have you killed. You see, our family has been growing. I have a lot of people fighting for the cause now, people who go back out into society, undercover. You'll never know if the next girl you pick up will be one of mine, one who will slit your throat without a second thought. That and the fact that two of your employees are members, members that will gladly take you out as well. That's right, don't look so shocked, that's how I got all the information on you. You see, the family will work with or without you. We will take back the world and make it a better place. With you would just be a lot easier.

Now, I'm going to take off the gag. I want to hear one word out of your mouth and one word only; either a yes or a no. Anything else and I will slit you from ear to ear. That a boy, no yelling. Now, what will your answer be...?

"Yes...." Good boy now let's go make the world a better place.

*\*Author's Note*
*This story is based on a very real cult that actually existed and did the sexual things in the story. The story of the young lady on the other hand is made up, though a real cult member did kill several*

*people, though they killed former members and himself out of revenge for such long abuse. There is no evidence that the cult is making a comeback or are responsible for any murders. Though there is no saying that this, couldn't be happening. Just be careful who you sleep with… it might be one of God's Whores.*

# MY LAST EMAIL ATTEMPT

Dear Friends and Family,

This is my last attempt. I have called all of you, spoken to some of you in person, and yet I am still sitting here. None of you would believe me. You all said I was nuts, that I needed help. Some of you even stopped taking my calls or answering my emails. I know what I'm telling all of you seems insane, but it is TRUE. And this just might be my last email. Maybe when it's over, when my life is over, then you'll all believe me.

You are all going to be angry with yourselves. You'll ask each other "why didn't we believe her?" Well it's too late for that now. For it is 2:32 A.M. Eleven minutes before it happens every night. I only hope that I can finish this email and send it off before it's too late. That way, there will be some sort of record of my last few minutes on this earth. I'm afraid this email will probably be the last thing I ever do, even though I *will* try my damnedest to live. I'm not going out without a fight. And that is why I feel as if I won't make it tonight. How can I fight something you can't touch, especially when you don't understand what it is? How do you prepare for the unknown? What weapons can you use on something that is not alive? I don't have answers to these questions. And that is why I don't think my fight will last long. It will be more than any of you have done though. If just ONE of you listened, if just ONE of you helped, maybe then we could have stopped this, together. And if I don't stop it, who knows what will happen. Will it move on to others? Will it stop? I have no answers but I pray it will end with me.

Please believe me.

As I am writing this, I am sitting on the floor Indian style in the living room, with my laptop on my lap, facing the spare bedroom door. I have shut and locked it. At least that way when it begins I will have some warning as the door opens. When it starts to jiggle or move is when I will hit send, so if I get cut off, just know that is what happened.

Please believe me.

Eight minutes left. I guess the main reason for this email is to let you all know that if I end up dead, I DID NOT kill myself. I can't stress that enough. If my suspicions are right, it will look as if I have done something to myself when they find my body in the morning. But no matter what the police say, one of you must fight for me. You all failed me in life, I beg of you, don't fail me in death as well. Tell the police I did not kill myself. From my other emails and our conversations you all know the story of what happens between 2:43 and 2:51 in my house. I don't have the time or energy to write about it all here again. One of you must have kept my email explaining it, use it as evidence in my case. Get a research team, have them come in and spend the night. For if I can't stop this thing, someone has to…or we'll all be horribly sorry.

You have to believe me.

Five minutes left. I can't hold back the tears. I just hope it doesn't know tears are a sign of weakness. It's a horrible feeling knowing you might die in a matter of minutes. I want to tell all of you that I love you, but you all know that, and it doesn't change the fact that I might die because none of you loved me enough to believe me. FOR CRYING OUT LOUD! Why couldn't just one of you had faith in me, humored me even? Damn it…I never wanted to die alone.…

You have no choice but to believe me.

It's getting colder in here now. I can see my breath starting to form small clouds in front of me. That always happens as it comes, as it makes its way out of that room. It means my time is almost up. I have to prepare. Next to me I have every item a cheesy Hollywood movie would suggest I should have in a situation like this. Though I know they will do nothing. The biggest weapon I have tonight is my courage to face it, to not run like I usually do. Every night I run screaming out of the house. Several times I almost didn't make it. I showed you all the bruises. You know the ones you all said I must have done to myself in my sleep. Well, you'll see tomorrow that I didn't.

Then you'll believe. Then you'll be sorry.

Light is starting to pour out from the cracks around the door. That means I have less than a minute. This is it…the moment of truth. If I live, you will all receive an email from me by 3:30 A.M. If not, I'm dead, call the police and have them come to my house and please one of you come as well to be witness to what you could have stopped.

God, my heart is pounding, I'm on my knees now so I can stand up quickly. The door handle just moved.

Rick put the email that he printed a few minutes earlier down. With a deep breath and sip of his coffee, he decided to go over to his sister's house to see if she was alright. She hadn't answered the phone, but he knew she was just trying to scare all of them. She needed help, no one in the family wanted to admit it though. They all just ignored the fact and pushed it aside, ignored her. Well, today he'd take care of it all. Go over there, make sure she didn't hurt herself and then drive her to the hospital so she could check herself in for observation. It wouldn't be easy, but at least he'd have done his part and he could go back to his life with no more calls at three in the morning.

An hour later, Rick was banging on his sister's door to no avail. With a heavy sigh, he looked at his key ring, trying to figure out which one was the spare she gave him a year ago when she moved into this dump of a house. She called it a "fixer upper". She was going to make it nice and sell it for a profit, just like on one of those shows. Only a month after she lived there, she started to complain about noises and things happening. Everyone humored her at first, but then it got annoying and people started to ignore her. Especially after her dinner party that was supposed to prove to everyone that stuff was happening. The only thing that happened was his sister throwing a fit, screaming at everyone and breaking dishes. That was the turning point. Most everyone gave up, Rick included, but he had to check on her now, she was his sister after all.

After four failed attempts, Rick found the right key and opened the door with ease. The kitchen looked normal, nothing seemed to be wrong. He called her name out two, three times only to receive no answer. She was really playing hard to get this time. He was going to be so pissed if he found her sitting on the couch, trying to just prove a point to everyone that "something" could happen. Grabbing a green apple off the counter, he wiped it on his shirt, took a bite and headed for the living room. *Talk about a wasted Sunday morning.* Rounding the corner, Rick stopped in his tracks, but kept chewing. His sister was sitting on the couch, but what he saw was so unreal he couldn't do anything but freeze and finish his bite. After a dry, hard swallow, the realization sunk in, his sister *was* dead.

At first he was filled with anger, *how could she kill herself? How could she do that to me?* Then he saw that she hadn't died from any normal suicide he knew of. With a steady step closer, he saw her eyes were missing. Another step closer revealed that her eyes were sitting in the palms of her hands. It wasn't until he was close enough to lean in did he notice that something seemed to be wrong with her chest. She always had ample breasts, for some reason, she now had none. They were gone, but there was no blood on her shirt. *She, she couldn't have done this to herself.*

With the sight in front of him really not settling in, he heard a noise to his left, from behind the door she was so afraid of. *What is going on?* Rick found himself compelled to walk to the door, he didn't know if he needed to know what was behind it, or if he just needed to stop looking at his sister's body. Whatever the reason, he walked right towards the door without stopping. Putting his hand on the knob, he felt a tear come out of his eye. With one swift push, the door flew open. The moaning, growling sound he heard as the door hit the wall was unlike anything he had ever heard. What he saw was even worse.

"Dear god sis… I'm so, so sorry I didn't believe you."

# SCRUFF

Rubbing the bristles, she contemplated the best way to rid her life of the cursed hairs. Trim them with sheers before using a razor? She really didn't have a clue. She had never been allowed to get rid of the beard that made her famous. Since it started growing when she was fourteen she had never shaved it. A year after the growth started, soon as they realized that it wasn't going to go away, her parents sold her to Mr. Crimshaw. They had no use for a "freak" and with twelve kids it was better to make sixty bucks to get rid of one rather than have to feed its useless mouth. Those were the words she heard through the door as she listened to her father talk to the circus owner all those years ago. Since that day she had been traveling the country, virtually a prisoner of her own hormonal imbalance.

Trim them, definitely have to trim them first. The sheers she found were rusty, but they still worked. Ricardo used them to cut the canvas and ropes, it should cut the course hairs. Looking in the scratched up, discolored mirror, that she gave up a week's pay for, she grabbed the beard and pulled the end taut. Having never cut it, the thick matted hair was down to her waist. Mr. Crimshaw made her comb it and put a pink bow in the middle that matched the pink dress she had to wear when she went out to "perform", which really entailed sitting on a swing behind bars while people laughed and called her names. Most days she could ignore them and just hum to herself. She loved music, but hardly got to listen to

131

anything besides the repetitive organ music two tents over. Every once in a while the crew and performers would be allowed a free night. They would all gather around the fire and play various instruments. Most of them were not good at it, but it was wonderful. Oh so wonderful! Sela looked forward to those nights. She looked forward to any night she didn't have to sit in the cage.

The sheers hesitated half way up the beard. Could she really do this? As awful as her daily humiliating routine was, she had no other life. No family to go to. No friends to stay with. She'd be on her own. In truth, she didn't even know what happened in the real world. The only contact she had with it was through the people who walked by and mocked her. Mr. Crimshaw told her that outside of the circus it was cruel, worse than what she lived.

"They'd treat you like the animal you are out there! They'd ridicule and shun you. You'd be dead in a week if you tried to live like them. You belong here, with the other freaks. They, are your family." Those are the words that Mr. Crimshaw yelled at her the few times she mentioned leaving. He'd also laughed and laughed at her. She'd come back with a question.

"Well if I can't be one of them, then why do you pay me? I have never been able to spend a dime of it!" It was true. He paid her only pennies a week and usually deducted most of it for menial things like using too much toilet paper. Having never been able to use the money she didn't know that she was making less than an hour's worth of work for days on end in the cage. The real reason he paid her was so she didn't feel like a slave. That and in case the authorities investigated he had proof of paying his "employees".

Snip. Sela couldn't believe it, but she squeezed the sheer handles, cutting a good foot off of her beard. Even if she stopped now she was in big trouble. Mr. Crimshaw would beat her for hours. Never in the face though. That shows, and customers don't like to see bruises on the faces of freaks, no matter how scary they are. He'd probably be even rougher to her during her "duties", her daily task of bending over and exposing her rear to him so he could "relieve" himself. It was routine and usually she didn't mind it. It was better than being made fun of. Only when he was drunk would he punch her. Usually in the sides, over and over again, making her cry feverishly, but silently. She knew that if she objected, it would only be worse. When she'd bleed, which Mr. Crimshaw told her was God punishing her for Eve's sin on mankind, he would take a soda-pop, shake it up and spray it inside of her to cleanse her before he did his thing. Only being able to bathe once a week (if that, usually they had the opportunity only when they passed a pond or lake) the soda would usually dry on her thighs making them uncomfortably sticky for days. She hated the feeling of walking around all day with each thigh sticking to the other for a split second as they passed.

Holding the rough, dark tuft of hair in her hand she wanted to set it on fire. If it weren't for this, this meaningless hair, she would be normal. She'd be on the other side of the bars, she'd be the one calling out names. Though she was better than that. The other cages were filled with her friends. She knew them by their names, Sam, Tina, Rex, Digger and Marx. Not the Sword Swallower, The Fattest Woman in The World, The Smallest Man In The World and The Wolf Man. Unlike the horrible crowds she didn't see their 'freakiness," she only saw them. Her family. She would never dare call them names.

Letting the hair drop to the dirt ground of her tiny tent, she grabbed a few inches higher and placed the blades in position to cut again. As she went to close the blades she thought about Tina braiding her hair, Rex doing a dance to make her laugh, Sam picking her flowers by the lake and Marx confiding in her about how he knows what she goes through. This *was* her family. This was all she knew. The beard was all she had. She needed it to keep her family. She was going to stay. A smile started to cross her face. Things were going to be all right she whispered to herself as the tent flap flew back.

"What in damnation are you doing?" Mr. Crimshaw was early. He usually showed up for their nightly routine much later.... Sela learned from her years that when addressing Mr. Crimshaw to look at the floor and to say sir. Adverting her eyes to the filthy ground by her sleeping sack made her unable to see the blow that hit her in the gut. She doubled over, falling to her knees, yet she was able to keep the scissors in her hands. Mr. Crimshaw stormed passed her and picked up the tuft of hair on the ground.

"This! You see this?" Grabbing the hair on her head he pulled it back to show her the filthy hairs clenched in his fists.

"This is money! My money! People pay to see this shit!" Sela's scalp was on fire from the hairs being pulled. Every fiber in her body wanted to scream out in pain, but she held it in. She deserved the punishment anyway, she did do something stupid.

"I'll take…uh…a pay…cut" slipped from her lips.

"You're damn right you will, you'll never get paid again. And if you think that is all you'll get from this you're dead wrong! Now open your mouth!" Knowing what he was going to do, yet not daring enough to defy him, Sela opened her mouth. Not even halfway open, Mr. Crimshaw crammed the wad of hair deep into her mouth. Sela gagged instantly but he held her head so tightly she couldn't pull away. His dirt covered callused fingers pushed the hair further and further into her mouth and down her throat. He wasn't happy until his whole hand was lodged in her teeth unable to go any farther in.

"This is what wasted money tastes like. If you don't like it, you better not do anything like this again!" He spat in her face keeping his hand in her mouth. Sela didn't hear a word of it though. She was too busy concentrating on the air she wasn't getting. She sucked hard through her mouth but it only pulled the hair deeper down her throat, her nose was of no use either. She tried telling him with her eyes that she couldn't breathe. It didn't work, looking him in the eyes garnered a kick to the ribs, which made breathing even harder. She had two choices: die or live. Dying would be an escape from the hell she lived. But Mr. Crimshaw told her time and time again how she was going to Hell, making her more afraid of death than anything else in the world. She chose to live, and swung the sheers right into Mr. Crimshaw's face.

The crusty blades, clamped tightly together, glided right through his left eye on an angle, broke his nose and came out the right eye. Instantly Mr. Crimshaw released Sela and fell backwards. Sela fell forward ripping the hair out of her throat and vomited. It took her several minutes to get enough air in her lungs before she could even realize what she did. Gathering herself enough to crawl, she made her way over to Mr. Crimshaw. White, gooey ooze ran down his cheeks from his missing eyes. His nose was crooked with an odd lump pointing at her like an accusing finger. Yet he was not dead. His head lolled back and forth as his mouth opened and closed in rhythm with it. Though she already vomited, the sight of his face made her dry heave.

Knowing she needed help, she ran to Marx's tent, it was the closest. In seconds the two of them were back

135

standing over Mr. Crimshaw in awe, wondering what to do. Minutes after that Sam, Rex and Digger where standing over him as well. They knew he needed help to live, but they also knew that getting him help meant that Sela was going to get in trouble, especially if he lived. Maybe if they all didn't internally hate him they wouldn't have hesitated to get help. After a few minutes of confused silence Digger and Rex ran to Tina's tent and told her the news. She was the one that came up with the plan.

It was simple really. And no one objected to it. Simply wait a few hours, remove the scissors and pour some alcohol on him. Mr. Crimshaw was notorious for drunken nights. Then all they had to do was toss him into the tiger's cage. The trainer and Mr. Crimshaw were known for getting in bitter arguments about how Mr. Crimshaw would tease the tigers when he got drunk. Mr. Crimshaw would argue that they were animals and that it didn't matter. It would make sense for him to have accidentally fallen in the cage while drunk and teasing the tigers.

Sela stayed with Tina while the men went about the plan. Rex was the lookout. Sam and Digger carried Mr. Crimshaw's twitching body and Marx opened the cage. His body hit the ground with a dull thud, he didn't yell, and they were all thankful for that. Within seconds, three of the tigers were tearing into Mr. Crimshaw. Large chunks of skin and meat were being torn from his arms and legs, but he didn't scream or even try to fight them off. They only watched for a few seconds, none of them wanted to see it and they definitely didn't want to be around when he was found.

It was done with so quickly they all felt like nothing had happened. Afterwards, they sat around together and played cards like any other night... until the screaming started. Knowing it would happen, the gang, minus Tina, ran over to the ruckus, pretending to wonder what the fuss was about. Every member of the circus watched as Raul, the tiger trainer, cried while holding onto the bars of the cage. He wasn't crying for Mr. Crimshaw though, he was worried that one of his baby's would choke on a belt buckle or a shoe. It was then that Rex saw the sheers in the cage. He panicked for a quick second until Raul started to curse the heavens about how Mr. Crimshaw must have tried to cut the tigers hair. They'd all laughed about that for years.

By the time the tigers were done eating there was only bone and shreds of clothing left. The next day the circus ran like normal, the show must go on as they say. Sela was made fun of in her cage and patrons threw popcorn at her like always. Only at night, she didn't have to go through her routine and when Mr. Carl, who took over for Mr. Crimshaw came to pay her, she was given ten times what she made in a year, for her week's work. He even asked her if she wanted to go into town with the rest of the crew for dinner and shopping. Rubbing the scruff on her face, she held back tears and gladly accepted the invitation.

*Michael Gore*

# THE HUMAN DART BOARD
## (Inspired By True Events)

Darts is a masterful game. It takes patience, a steady hand, a good eye and a strong mind. It's a game that is not too common in the US, but very common in the UK. I'm not sure why. Personally I think it is better than bowling or golf, which I have no clue why are so popular here. I think they are god awful boring. I'm not going to go into why they are so horrible, because I'm sure you think them insufferable as well. Anyway, back to my story. So, I killed my grandmother when I was fifteen. She was reading a Dr. Seuss book to my little brother in the kitchen when I shot her. I really just wanted to see what it would be like to kill her, I had no other reasons.

Of course I was a bit stupid (hey I was kid), I didn't think about my grandpa! When he got home I killed him as well, didn't think I had any other choice. After that I went to a state hospital. It was alright, lot of freaking crazy people there though. Man they were nuts. That is where I fell in love with darts. No, they didn't give the crazy people darts, we were not allowed sharp objects. One of my doctors, Larry, had a board in his office. He said it helped him relax when he was stressed. He let me play with it one day and from there I was hooked! We started tournaments and played for hours when he should have been working. Great guy, he is also the one that signed the papers to let me out.

Anyway, am I boring you? I hope not, really hope not, I wouldn't want to do that to a guest. You know something, I don't even know why I'm telling you my life story, you probably know it anyway, right?  No?  Alright then, I'll keep going for a bit then, stop me if it gets boring.  Well, by the time I got out I was the height I am now, can you imagine being six foot nine and three hundred pounds at that age?  People didn't want anything to do with me.  Regardless, I got a job at the Public Works, boring shit.  Probably why I even started this shit, I just got so damn bored.  I picked up a hitchhiker one day for shits and giggles, ended up being more for shits.  I strangled her in the car, drove around for a while with her propped up with the seat belt.  Tell you what, that was a kick!  Sitting in traffic next to people, they had no clue she was dead, funny shit.

When I got her back here, we had some great sex, I mean amazing stuff.  She satisfied me like no living woman ever, ever could.  She was like Linda Lovelace for crying out loud!  Well when we were done, I cut her up, I think twelve pieces in all and dumped the body.  I knew from that day on that I had to keep doing that, it was a blast!

I did another five more the same way, though we'd try different things in bed each time and I killed a few differently for fun.  Oh, I even ate some of them.  Not much, just taste tests really.  Not bad actually.  I mean if I was any sort of cook, I probably could have made a hell of a meal.  Well that leads us, in a very short way, up to today.  So let's get to the matter at hand, the bitch.

For one thing I have no clue how you are friends with my mom, I mean, my whole life she has been nothing but a bitch.  Always yelling at me and shit.  Did I tell you what I did with her vocal cords?  No?  Well I cut them out and put them in the garbage disposal, but get this!  The fucking things flew back up at me!  Even when she was dead, she was still bitching at me!  I couldn't get her to shut up!

I really hope she felt every hit of that damn hammer,. I used the ball-peen hammer so it would hurt more. She didn't make much noise though, too bad. Well that brings us up to you. As you can see in front of you, I cut her head off and hung it up, so I could play darts. But then I realized, what fun is darts if you have no one to play against? So I figured, what the hell and called you up. Of course you panicked so I had to tie you up like this, but don't worry, I'm going to untie one hand so you can throw the darts. But don't get smart, you try to throw one at me, I'll eat your calf and keep you alive to watch me do it, got that? I hope that doesn't sound cruel, I mean I still want to be your friend and I hope we have a very competitive game, so let's get at it.

Alright, your arm good that way? Excellent. Here is the point method. The forehead is worth ten, the cheeks, twenty, chin, thirty, nose, forty and the eyeballs, fifty each! Oh and the lips are twenty-five. Sound good? I'll throw first, I have to warn you, I'm pretty good. Here we go. Damn it! Forehead, well that is ten for me. Your turn, here is the dart. Christ! Try it again, if you don't hit the head, it doesn't count. You missed again, are doing this on purpose? You are pissing me off! Hit the board or I'm eating your calf, I'm getting hungry anyway. There you go! Cheek, good job, you're in the lead. My turn. Jesus! Did you see how the eye just popped like that, goddamn, fifty for me! You better try hard to catch up, I forgot to tell you, if you lose, we use your head next. And sadly for you, I have a feeling that I'm going to win.

\*\*Note from the author. While this story is fiction, the man and the actions the character do in this story are more than real. The killer's name was Edmund Kemper and the line, "Even when she was dead, she was still bitching at me! I couldn't get her to shut up!" was a really line he told the police about when his mother's vocal cord came out of the garbage disposal.

# HOME LIPOSUCTION

Patty was awake. She stared at the ceiling and listened to John's rhythmic snoring. Part of the snore was soothing. The other part grated on her nerves. If she didn't know better, she would have thought he did it on purpose. Just like he got fat on purpose. Rolling over she stared at the massive mound next to her. John was three, maybe four times the size he was when she married him. She had been trying for two years to get him to lose weight. He would always just laugh and say he was comfortable in his new plump size. She brought him flyers on diet systems, books, pills, detoxes and even surgery options. John would throw them all away. Staring at the mound, Patty knew it was time to take matters into her own hands.

Patty looked at John's hip and ass as he lay on his side facing away from her. It was like a mountain. The night before, Patty got a measuring tape and measured the width of his ass while he slept. It was over forty inches wide. It disgusted her. She worked so hard to keep herself healthy. Five work outs a week, diets and even pills. She didn't like to brag but she looked damn good for a woman over fifty. Hell, all the ladies at the country club always told her how jealous they were of her body. Whenever anyone mentioned John though, she would panic and get fluttered. "John? Oh, he is fine, fine. He actually started a new diet plan. Exercising like a fool. Hopefully it will work, you know that stupid glandular problem he has is such a pain." And this would be her response to a simple, "How is John?"

A week ago Patty looked up liposuction. It would be a quick solution to getting John back to a weight where she could go out with him in public again. She *was* going to book it without telling him, then trick him into getting it done. That is until she saw the price. If it were two years ago she would have plunked the money down like it was nothing. But after John's bad turn in the stock market last year, she had to scrimp every dime they could to keep up the appearance that they were still doing well. She had to even charge the $30,000 yearly fee for the country club to a credit card, which was embarrassing. Things were sure to turn around soon… they had to. That was another reason to get John thin. She believed if he were thin again, he would get his confidence back. With his confidence, he could get their money back.

John stirred a bit and for some reason it annoyed Patty. She loved the man, she did, but he repulsed her at the same time. She just knew if he lost the weight she would be able to love him again. That is why she made a plan…

Looking at the clock, she sighed. Though she was ready to do it, she was still nervous. The plan was to start at ten-thirty, but she gave herself a few extra minutes to mentally prepare and got out of bed just before eleven. John was a pretty heavy sleeper so she wasn't nervous about waking him up as she prepared the items she needed, that would be the easy part. The hard part would be tying him down without waking him up.

With everything next to the bed that she needed, she carefully slipped the covers off over John's feet. She had pre-tied four double nooses out of silk sheets. She secured all four to the bedposts and let the other loops hang by John's limbs. Now all she had to do was slip them on to him before he awoke. She knew the feet would be easier so she started with them. The first one went on without a hassle. John rolled a bit as she tried to put on the other one, but she got it without him waking up. Thankfully, John was on his back when she went for his right hand. As she carefully lifted it John moaned something that sounded like a mix between a baby sucking a pacifier and a duck being crushed. As she pulled his arm above his head tightening the loop she saw his eyes start to flutter. Racing around the bed she grabbed John's other hand, slipped the rope around it and pulled it tight as he awoke.

"Wha…Pat?" Patty shushed John and rubbed his head.

"Don't worry honey, I just want to play a little game. I figured we haven't woken up in the middle of the night to do… *this,* in a long time." Seeing a smile cross his face, she knew there would be a small rise under his belly in a few seconds.

"What has gotten into you baby, we haven't had sex in ages?" He said through squinted eyes. Patty seductively rubbed his chest.

"Now be a good boy and open your mouth." Through the darkness she could see his quizative expression, but he did as she asked. She fumbled a bit but, she got the ball gag on him rather quickly. She bought it online from a sex website since there was no way she would risk being seen in the local filth shop. She figured it would be more comfortable for John than a piece of cloth, besides, he needed something soft to bite down on.

"Grmulb. Ohgoodo." John gurgled as he tried to talk through the gag. Patty ignored the grumbles and pulled off the bed sheets. There was John, spread eagle in all his glory, naked. The sight sent a shudder down her spine. She did her best to never look at John naked. The lights were off on the rare occasion they had sex and when he walked around naked after a shower she avoided looking at him. Seeing him this way now, she knew why she was doing this.

"John, I'm sorry, you are not getting laid tonight." Patty barked as she flipped on the light switch. John's eyes fluttered and filled with panic. Patty kept her focus on them instead of his massive gut. Even then she could see in her peripheral his pudgy erection shrinking. John mumbled more and pulled at the restraints a bit.

"Listen honey, I love you, always have. But you don't listen to me and I don't think you ever will. I have been so supportive for years with your weight. I have tried everything I can think of to get you to lose it. You wouldn't do any of it. You *never* even tried one thing I suggested." Patty walked around the bed and set up a few work lights she bought at Home Depot. Flicking them on she saw that John could hardly keep his eyes open, which was a good thing, he didn't need to see this.

"Look, baby, I'm not letting you ruin your life… and *mine* by getting even bigger. Your blood pressure is up, your cholesterol is high. You are going to die if you don't get some of the weight off of you. That's why I'm doing this, to give you a quick fix…. I hope that once you get some of the weight off, that it will motivate you to change your ways." John kicked a bit and tried to pull at the ties.

"Sweetie, you have to be very, very still for what I'm about to do. It's already going to hurt like hell. If you move… it might kill you." Suddenly the thrashing stopped.

"Huuuugh? Huuuugh?" John tried to ask. Patty patted his large stomach watching the ripples jiggle their way through his fat. The thought of the massive stomach

145

being gone in a few minutes gave her the courage to look at it.

"I watched the videos online a hundred times. I have prepared everything to be sanitary and as safe as possible. I just need you to do your part and everything will be alright. And your part is the easiest, it's just being still." Patty stood up, grabbed some rubber gloves off of the nightstand and put them on. She could hear John's breathing speed.

"I bought some pain killers online, from Canada. I'll give them to you after the operation. I'm afraid if I take your gag off now I won't be able to get it back on you. So the better you are, the less you move, the quicker I'll get you some pain pills." She heard a sniffle and looked at John's face. His eyes were starting to get watery. She looked away immediately and started preparing her tools.

Laid out next to the bed she had rubbing alcohol, cotton swabs, a long, thin, hard plastic tube, a small box cutter, duct tape, a plastic cap with a hole in it, gauze pads and bandages for after the surgery. Next to her legs was the brand new wet/dry shop vacuum she bought along with the work lights; top of the line, strongest sucking power. She grabbed the long black tube of the vacuum and fitted the plastic cap over it. Using the duct tape she sealed it on tight. Next she fitted the plastic tube into the hole of the cap and taped that as well. Next she took a cotton swab, covered it in alcohol and wiped down the tube. She tossed the swab on the floor, got another one, and doused it in alcohol.

"I'm going to start with your stomach, the most fat is there." Patty rubbed the alcohol swab right over his hip like she had seen in the online videos. Throwing the swab on the floor she grabbed the box cutter and held it to the cleansed area. John started to kick.

"Damn it John! Don't move, I can totally screw you up if you do. I'm serious. I know what I'm doing. I practiced. I filled a plastic bag with Jell-O and sucked it out. I did perfect." John stopped moving and settled down a bit. She looked at his face, it was filled with fear, it was a look she had never seen on him before. The look hurt her, but she knew she was doing this for his own good.

With one quick swipe she cut an inch long slit in his side. John buckled and fell flat back on the bed.

"Okay, okay, good. Good John, now is the important part, stay still, I'm going to put the tube in you and turn on the vacuum. Before you know it you'll be fifty pounds lighter!" Using two fingers she spread the cut open. Blood poured out over her gloves but she was fine with that, she planned on getting new sheets and a mattress when this was over. With her free hand she grabbed the hose. She could feel John starting to tremble under her hand. She calmly shushed him and hummed as she lined the tube up with the open hole. She hesitated, but then slowly slid it in.

"It's in baby, it's in. I'm going to turn on the vacuum now, don't move." She purposely avoided eye contact with him as she reached back and flipped the switch on. The motor revved. Patty waited patiently praying to herself that it would work, it had to. After a few seconds the hose jumped slightly followed by a loud sucking, slurping sound. Patty's eyes widened as she watched the tube fill with a bloody, beige liquid. As the fat hit the vacuum's holding tank she could hear wet slapping noises.

"It's working!" John screamed through his gag and writhed, but she didn't let it faze her, it was working. As the flow started to slow, Patty moved the tube back and forth until it started to shake with suction again.

147

John's body shook and he cried profusely, but he had stopped moving. Patty pushed on the outside of the body, coaxing the fat towards the tube. She could see the tip moving around under his skin, the fat puckering up, then indenting and disappearing.

After a few minutes his stomach was half the size. The only problem was the fat Patty removed was only from John's left side, his right side still bulged. As she unplugged the vacuum and wheeled it around to the other side she caught a glimpse of the lopsided stomach. It was freakish looking, the sight made her stomach roll. Regardless, she started the process over and began to suck on the right side. As the lumpy mound started to disappear she heard an odd whining sound coming from the vacuum. Flipping it off she lifted the vacuum up a bit to feel the weight.

"Wow. It's full already John! This is amazing. You are going to look so good. I'll go empty it and then I'll get to work on your thighs." As she pushed the vacuum out of the room she could hear John whimper behind her. It hurt her, but she knew when he saw himself in the mirror, he would be kissing her he'd be so happy. As she reached the top of the stairs she tried to lift the vacuum. It was a bit heavier than she had planned. Putting it back down, she thought about dumping it in the bathroom. She decided against it, she didn't want to overflow the toilet and she didn't want the fat clogging the shower drain either. The thought of a plumber coming in and pulling out gobs of fat made her realize that dumping it outside in the woods was her only option. With a deep breath she tried lifting it again. This time she was able to get it up enough to start down the stairs.

The steps were slippery in socks; the expensive hardwood was highly polished. Patty was thankful she had her sneakers on to give her good footing. Her footing didn't matter though, since her arms gave out. The vacuum landed on her feet, tipped forward, and fell. Patty reached for it, but wasn't fast enough. As the vacuum tipped over the top fell off sending two gallons of fat and blood pouring down the stairs. Patty let out a scream as she watched the waterfall of beige and pink gobs pour down each step, fall off the sides and finally land on the ten thousand dollar carpet at the base of the stairs. Her first reaction was to race down the stairs and move the carpet. The stairs could be cleaned, but the carpet could not. Holding the railing tight she took one step, her foot didn't slip so she felt confident in going faster. She was wrong. On her third step her foot shot out from under her and banged its way down four stairs while her other foot stayed locked in place. Her grip on the railing wasn't tight enough and she ended up doing the splits. Almost instantly she felt her groin muscles snap. As she reached down to grasp her thighs that were burning she lost the last support she had and she fell over. As she tumbled down the stairs she felt the warm fat slide against her skin, go up her nostrils, fill her ears and mouth, it tasted salty on her lips and burned in her eyes.

Lying on the now worthless carpet she didn't move, she let the pain wash over her along with the rest of the fat that was dripping down. Her head, back, elbows and groin all ached in unison as she spat the gobs of goo from her lips. As she started to test each limb to see if she could move, she heard noises upstairs. She wanted to shout up to John to tell him she was going to be a few minutes but her head hurt too much. The noises kept coming, then she realized they were footsteps, John's? Patty tilted her throbbing head and looked to the top of the stairs. The steps kept coming and sure enough, it was John. He stood at the top of the stairs, naked, dripping blood and goo from his sides. His stomach was deflated and loose, it looked un-proportioned to the rest of his body, like some sort of blow up doll with only the torso deflated.

"Baby. You should lie down, you don't look good. I'll be fine, I don't think I broke anything just pulled my groin, it's hard to get up, but I'm alright…. How did *you* get up?"

"You could never tie knots for shit." Patty gave him a smile as she watched him grab both railings before taking slow steady steps down.

"Honey, you should lay down, the stairs are very slippery, and you need your rest." Patty tried to sit up but the pain in her head made her lay back down. She tried several more times to talk John out of coming down the stairs, but he wouldn't stop. Steady, slow step after step he came down.

"I can get up on my own baby, don't worry about me." John didn't say anything when got to the carpet. Patty looked up at him, the view was hideous. The loose skin of his stomach was slimy from the blood and fat dripping out, it hung over his penis, only his bulbous hairy balls hung down below it.

"Just give me an hour and we'll do the rest, you are already looking great." Patty reached up to give him her hand for help up, but he walked past it. Turning the other way she saw him putting the vacuum upright.

"Honey, I'll do that, don't worry about it." Patty whispered as John bent over, grabbed the power cord and plugged it in. She was starting to get worried, what was he doing? She forced herself to sit up as she couldn't stand up for the life of her. She propped herself against the stairs and felt a bit better now that she could see what John was doing. As she watched John's fat seep through her shirt she felt sticky and gross, she wanted to shower, but she had to help John finish. As John picked up the hose she saw the end of the plastic tube had cracked off, it was jagged and sharp.

"Oh, baby, it broke. It's all right, I have an extra one upstairs. We'll have to switch it before we finish. Let's get cleaned up and take some pain pills. Then we…" The sound of the vacuum turning on drowned out her voice. She was terrified that John had snapped, that he was so excited about losing weight that he was going to stick the tube in himself and keep working at it. She yelled over the hum for him to shut off the vacuum, but John didn't acknowledge her. Instead he turned towards her and smiled.

"Tit, for tat…baby." John screamed over the vacuum. Patty suddenly realized what he was doing. John reached down to her, she tried to fight off his grip, but her elbows were aching and she could put up no fight at all. John lifted her shirt and plunged the jagged edge of the tube in her stomach. The pain was immediate and searing, but it was nothing compared to the feeling of her intestines being pulled out of her body. Purple chunks being sucked through the tube were the last thing she saw.

# REFRIGERATOR POETRY

The first time it happened I didn't think much of it. Maybe I was drunk and moved the words around or maybe Danielle did it before…. well just before. Hundreds of tiny magnetic words. Part of a stupid ass magnetic poetry thing that Danielle put on the fridge to "lighten up" the place. It annoyed me when she first put it there. But I learned to just ignore it, not like I needed the space on the fridge anyway. It was two days after, when it happened… when I noticed the sentence. How I didn't notice it before, I have no clue. I was reaching in to get another Bud when it caught my eye. On the freezer door, where all those damn little words were spread out, was a sentence; *The Water Is Too Low*. I read it four or five times. I even finished half of my beer standing there trying to figure out what it meant. Was Danielle leaving me a note? Was it supposed to be some sort of lyric or whatever those stupid poem things are called? Whatever it was, I gave up trying to figure it out. I took my dry cracked hand and swirled the magnets around to get rid of the message.

The second time it showed up, well, I panicked. Once again I was getting a beer, and once again, a sentence was there. Before even reading it I dropped the can and ran to the sliding door on the balcony. It was locked. The five windows this piece of shit apartment had were all locked and the front door was secured from the inside. Besides the closet, which I checked, there is no place to hide. I knew I was alone and that whoever did

152

this must have done it in the small window of time that I ran to the liquor store to stock up on chips and beer. How they got in and out, I have no clue. A bit calmer, I went to the fridge to read the sentence: *Evidence Everywhere No Way Out.* I picked the beer can up off the floor, popped it open and downed it in four gulps. I needed something harder if I was to deal with this. Someone knew what happened. Someone saw me. And now they were trying to fuck with me? What did they want? Money? Good luck getting that. Shit I can't even make rent this month with Danielle gone and all.

Slugging down another beer I thought of who could have seen me. It did take me three trips. I mean, is four trash bags, that suspicious? I guess when you put them in your car at 4:00 a.m. it is. But that is why I waited so late. I went for a walk before hand and made sure every light was off in the complex. I thought no one was up. Unless... it was the old bitch. The one always sitting at her window no matter what time of the day it is. She must have been up with the light off just staring out! That's it! But how could she get in my apartment? I've never even seen her walk, let alone outside of her apartment. It didn't matter, it had to be her and I had to do something about it.

Six beers later it was almost two in the morning and I was ready to get to the bottom of this. I grabbed one of the spare pillowcases that Danielle used to throw a fit about if I threw it on the floor, *they get wrinkled.* Inside of it I stuck a bunch of my socks and left the apartment. I looked around and once again I saw no lights on, so I knocked on her door while looking over my shoulder. It took a solid four hard knocks until she answered. I didn't know her name since I had never met her, but I had a plan. The door creaked open a bit; I made sure the bag was nestled under my arm gently.

"Ma'am, I know it's late, I'm sorry, but I think I found one of your cats outside." Without a word, the door shut and reopened.

"You put my cat in a bag? What is wrong with you mister?" It was the break I needed. Hard as I could, I lifted my leg and kicked the bitch in her chest, she went flying into the apartment. With another quick look over my shoulder, I went in after her and locked the door. She moaned and rolled, obviously confused at what just happened. I didn't want to hurt her, but she couldn't have more than a few months of life left anyway... so what the hell. I knelt down beside her and got into her face.

"Why are you fucking with me lady?" I'm not an angry person so I was impressed at how pissed I sounded when I screamed. Her eyes fluttered and her mouth gaped open before she answered with a moan.

"What do you mean?" I slapped her hard, twice. She closed her eyes.

"You saw me with the bags huh? You know what I did. And now what, you want my money? You disgust me!" I must say, she was a good actress. Tears were streaming down her face and she said she saw nothing. Not believing her, knowing, just knowing she would tell the police if I let her live, I crammed the pillowcase into her face. Compared to Danielle, she was remarkably easy to finish off. It only took a minute or so before she stopped fighting, but I kept the pillow pushed hard against her for an extra few.

Standing up I wasn't happy about what I had done, but at least I knew I didn't have to worry anymore. Looking around I was comfortable with the fact that it looked like no one was here. The cops would probably think she had a heart attack which meant I didn't have to do anything, no disposing of the body or cleaning up of anything. I simply looked out the window, made sure no one was around and slipped out of the apartment and back to mine.

I needed another beer.

Walking towards the fridge I almost fainted. Once again there was a sentence arranged out of those stupid fucking magnets. It wasn't her then…. Looking around the apartment I knew no one was there. I took a few steps toward the fridge and squinted in the darkness to read the sentence.

*Two In One Week, Tsk Tsk.* I was furious. I had to find this person fast. I needed to think about who could have seen me, but my full bladder was distracting my mind. I shuffled into the bathroom to take a piss. Flicking on the light I jumped backwards, terrified at what I saw; blood, everywhere. The shower stall was dripping from top to bottom. Smudges covered the walls, toilet and the floor was practically a pool. Just like it was the other night. I couldn't help but get Danielle's blood everywhere. It's almost impossible not to when you use a handsaw to cut a body up. But it couldn't be her blood. I washed it all away, scrubbed it, and bleached every inch of the room. Whose was it now? This fucker had to kill someone himself to cover the room like this! Shit, who the hell is this?

Backing away from the room I checked my hands and arms for blood. Luckily there was none. This guy was setting me up, that's what he was doing. He probably spread the blood and called the cops! I had to clean it up again before they got here. Killing the witness was more important though. Calming myself with another beer I thought long and hard about each window that had a view of my truck. There were only four apartments that could see my door and/or my truck. Mine, the old bitches, the hot young chick (whose car I didn't see the night I took out the body parts), and the Super. That's it. It's him! Of course. I'm such an idiot. He could easily slip in and out of my apartment, he has all the keys.

I had to search around for a while in the closet but I found my Dad's old hunting knife, it should do the job with ease. Hell, the Super is an old fuck. He must be over sixty and lives alone. About to close the closet door I took a second to visit Danielle. I did miss her. That's why I couldn't have let her leave me, I would have missed her too much. The box was up on the top of the shelf. I almost dropped it, but luckily caught it on my knee. Placing her down on the floor I pulled back the lid and saw her beautiful face staring up at me. She was starting to turn an odd color and smelled a bit but she was still beautiful. Sitting on the floor I fingered her mouth and thought about how she used to love sucking on my finger. I used to caress her lips until she would take my finger into her mouth whirling her tongue around it. It turned me on like no one's business. Even now I was starting to feel a tingle in my dick. For a split second I thought about taking down the box with her right breast (it was the bigger one) and her vagina so I could get off, but thought twice about it, I had work to do.

After putting Danielle back, I tucked the knife into my pant line. It felt awkward and I was worried it would fall and cut my leg open so I decided to hold it behind my back. Racing down the three flights to the bottom floor apartment labeled "Super", I was excited to finally have this shit end. I rang his buzzer (he was the only apartment that had one, I asked him once if we could get one and he said no, what a dick). Minutes later he opened the door in an old brown ragged robe as he squinted his eyes. Unlike the old hag, he opened his door right up.

"Apartment 3A, right? What ya need? Better be an emergency at this hour."

"Oh yes definitely, the fire sprinkler went off in the bathroom and won't stop, it's going to flood the whole place."

"No shit? Give me two seconds to grab my tools I'll be right there." As he turned around, I plunged the knife into the back of his neck. I was surprised how I could feel the bone grind against the blade. I thought it would have just slipped right in and out, instead it sort of got stuck. I couldn't even pull it out until he was on the floor. Thankfully I must have hit his vocal cord for he couldn't scream. When I went to shut the door I realized he was in the way of it. Panicking I looked behind me, having not before I attacked him. Thankfully, no one was there. Dragging him into the room I realized I was stupid to act so quick. He had gotten blood everywhere. On the carpet, on the floor and some had sprayed on the wall. Cleaning this up was going to be too much work. About to scratch my face, I realized I had blood all over me as well.

"You asshole! You bled on me!" I screamed at him as he flopped around like a fish out of water. To finish him off I stomped once, with all my strength, right onto his throat. His head stuck in an odd angle and he stopped moving. Not wanting to cut him up and dispose of him (time was running out as it was) I raced to the kitchen and found a notepad and pen and scrawled on it *"See if you cheat on me again dick head!"* It was genius, the cops would find that and think his girlfriend killed him. Hell, I don't even know if he has one, actually that would be even better because they will always be looking for her. Perfect plan.

A bit relaxed, I headed up to my apartment as the sun was just coming up. I should have enough time to clean up the bathroom and get into bed before any cops showed up to question me. I'll just tell them I was in my apartment all night with Danielle and that she left early this morning to go on a trip out of the country and that she'll be gone for a while. It'll work like a charm.

Back inside I stripped naked and headed right into the bathroom. It took a while but I got all the blood cleaned up. The apartment smelled like bleach again so I opened up the balcony door and turned on the ceiling fan to air out the place. Satisfied with my work I took a shower and put on some shorts and a t-shirt. I was ready to hit the hay but my stomach wasn't, it was growling at me. There was some left over pizza in the fridge so I went to go get a slice, I could eat it in bed. This time as I approached the fridge, I almost pissed myself. Another message was there, this time there was more, it was a poem.

> *Roses Are Red*
> *Violets Are Blue*
> *You Killed Me*
> *Now I'll Kill You*

Danielle. It was her, I knew it! She must have been getting out of the box when I wasn't paying attention. *She wasn't dead.* I knew she was still alive, I just knew it. I ran to the closet pulled her down and ripped open the box. There she was, she didn't look any different but I knew now that she was playing with me.

"Enough joking around honey. I know it was you. You really tricked me. I killed two people for crying out loud...." There was a knock on the door. It was the police, it had to be. Though I knew she was alive, I still hid her head back in the closet and opened the door. Two plain-clothes detectives greeted me with a smile. I didn't catch their names. My heart was beating too loud in my ears. I invited them in anyway.

"We are questioning everyone in the complex, your Super was murdered this morning." One of them said, I grunted some sort of response but a noise in the closet distracted me. Danielle was trying to get off the shelf to tell them what I did. Shit. What was I to do? She was angry I got rid of her body, she loved her body. She was going to have them take me to jail. I can't go there.

"Awfully early to be cleaning isn't it? Your place reeks of bleach sir. What were you cleaning up at such an hour?"

"Where were you last night?" The other asked me as I backed up to the closet. They were giving me an odd look, they had to hear her too. She was making a racket in there. She had to have been knocking the box back and forth trying to knock herself to the floor. This was it, what could I do?

"You feeling alright sir?" Before I could answer there was a loud "thump". The two looked at each other, they were going to search the closet, I just knew it.

"Sir, can we ask you to sit on the couch please while we look around your place?" I stepped away from the closet and thought for a split second about the knife, I hid it in the couch cushion in case I needed it. I could attack them. But they had guns. I was going to jail. NO. I can't. I'll die in there and I'll never see Danielle again.

"It's just my dog, he is in the closet, let me let him out." Opening the door I could tell the cops were suspicious, they had their hands on their guns. I couldn't believe it, but the box was still on the shelf and she seemed to not be moving now. Pulling it down I ignored their shouts to not touch the box and turned around to show it to them.

"It's just my dog." I repeated as they aimed their guns at me and yelled for back up. As I walked towards them they circled around me, leaving a straight line to the balcony open. It was my one chance to be with Danielle forever. If I jumped down I could run to my truck and get away. We could start a new life together! Other officers were entering my apartment but it was too late, they wouldn't catch me. I was already running full speed like a plane down a runway towards the door. With one swift leap I hurled myself over the railing. I was going to be free... I was going to be starting my new life with Danielle soon.

# STARING INTO INFINITY

Claire started off by taking an energy shower. She mixed salt, almond oil and sandalwood into a thick paste and rubbed it all over her body. It was coarse and grated against her skin painfully, but she savored the pain knowing it was washing away all the bad. The smell was strong, she took deep breaths of it, letting the good energy into her body. Rinsing in the cold water made her body shiver as she asked it to take away the bad energy. In theory, the bad energy along with the salt concoction was being washed down the drain.

Toweling off she felt alone in the house, for the first time since the incident. It was completely silent. No friends or family there to console her, no radio turned up loud to stop her mind from playing tricks on her in the silence. While the silence was irritating her, she did her best to focus on the task at hand, the ritual. If she let her mind stray it might not work. And if that happened she'd have to give up. She'd have to leave the house for good.

Following the directions, she put on light clothing, white cotton pajamas that Tim had bought her for her last birthday. She had removed all of her jewelry before the shower, except for her wedding ring. She now *had* to take it off, with a sigh, she thought about how it had never left her finger in the eleven years of her marriage. It took some effort but once it was off it felt like she had removed her whole finger. The skin under the ring was pale and sickly looking. Looking down at her hand with the ring off it didn't look like her own.  She forced the thoughts out of her mind and kept on with the process.

So far things were working, she thought.  Claire hated being barefoot, but for the ritual, she had to remain that way.  And even though it was in the thirties outside, she had to leave several windows open in the house; to let the negative air escape.  Walking to the front door her feet screamed at her as she crossed the frigid tile hallway floor.  She had already placed out the candles.  The first one was in the living room, the room where most of the negative energy was.  She had to light that one first.  Then, from room to room, she lit each candle.  If possible she was supposed to look back at the last candle as she lit the next.  This was hard to do and in most rooms it was impossible.  Room after room she lighted the hundred percent beeswax candles.  They could *only* be beeswax.  The first floor was done, she left one on the staircase and lit up the ones upstairs.  Putting some in the attic and basement crossed her mind but the directions didn't mention them, so she didn't bother.

With all the candles lit she made her way back into the living room and took a seat on the floor.  One solo candle sat in front of her.  Six inches high, three inches thick and white, the flame threw shadows all over the walls.  She was scared and that didn't help.  But she did her best to remain calm.  If she panicked, said a word or did one thing wrong it wouldn't work.  And it had to.

The next part she had figured out how to do during the day.  Stand up mirrors are hard to find in the store.  So instead she bought two square entryway mirrors that were each about three feet high and two feet wide with gold frames.  She had to place a dozen books in a stack to stand each mirror upright on the floor.  After some practice, she found the best way to set down each mirror.  The candle was now in the middle of the book stacks that were about four feet apart from each other. Taking in a few deep breaths she could still smell the salt on her skin as she set the first mirror in place. The light in the room increased as it reflected the candle off it. Trembling slightly she picked up the next mirror and put it in place.

When you place two mirrors in front of each other you create eternity. A reflection of a reflection. Never ending. When you place the candle in the middle of the two candles the light will illuminate each doorway into eternity. When eternity is opened up, the gateway will then suck the negative energy out of the room and send it into eternity, ridding your house of the bad for good. Or that is how it is supposed to work...according to Russian folklore at least. What Claire didn't know is that other religions and sects use this method to contact the dead... when you look into eternity you can see the sprits, of the past. For eternity stretches forever in time.

With everything set, the next step was for Claire to leave the room and let the candles work their magic. She didn't leave the room immediately though. A fatal mistake that the handbook did not warn her off. Instead Claire was nervous that the placement wasn't *just right*, so she leaned into the mirrors and looked to the left to make sure they were lined up to see eternity. She was fascinated by what she saw... doorway after doorway with no end to it. Each one lightly lit up with a thousand of her own faces looking blankly back at her.

Having never seen such a sight, she couldn't look away. It was beautiful, mysterious and mystical. Curious at the image looking back at her she moved her hand into view and waved to herself. An endless ray of her hands waved back and she giggled ever so slightly like a baby first discovering a mirror. She even smiled a bit. The task at hand was miles away from her mind...and that is when something else came into view. It was another hand, but not hers. Millions of identical hands popped up grabbing the doorframe of eternity. She felt a scream in her gut but held it back as she tossed off the image as her imagination. When a rough voice spoke, she knew it was all too real.

"Claire..." Echoed as if off a canyon and came out of the mirror. If it had been a stranger's voice she would have immediately backed up and ran out of the house screaming. But it wasn't. It was Tim's. Squinting harder at the hand she noticed the ring on it...Tim's wedding ring. Her heart started to thump with love as she realized her husband was trying to make contact with her. She had missed him horribly in the past month... since she killed him. It was deemed an accident, but only she knew the truth. Well her and Tim that is. They were painting the ceiling and Tim was nit picking at her like usual. She wasn't doing it right, what was her problem? Couldn't she do anything right? He was a good husband in all aspects, except for that one. He just never realized how demoralizing he could be with his comments. That day she just couldn't handle them. She had a bad week, she was already in a bad mood... so she pushed the ladder.

She was just angry; a push out of frustration seemed harmless. Not for a second did she think it would hurt him, let alone kill him. But it did. His foot got caught in the rung sending him backwards toward the fireplace. The ornate brass frame with the pointy tip that held up the mesh screen went right through the back of his head. It only took him a few seconds to die, as he did, he gave Claire a look that would never leave her mind, not even for a second. It was the same look he had now on his face as he peered around the edge of the doorframe and looked at her. Though there were millions of her hand, his hand and her head, there was only one of his head.

"I'm so, sorry…" Claire couldn't believe the ceremony was giving her a chance to apologize, a chance to redeem herself. It was much more than she could have ever hoped for. Hearing the words, Tim smiled slightly and shook his head no. Claire didn't understand the meaning. *No, don't blame yourself? No, it's not alright?* Leaning in closer to try to see him better she knocked over the candle. It went out. She couldn't see Tim anymore or even her own hand in the mirror. It was pitch black.

"No, no…Tim!" As she scrambled about to right the candle and find the lighter she felt a subtle pressure on her shoulder. It stopped her in her tracks. Looking in the mirror in front of her, she could see the hand coming out of the mirror. Then suddenly, violently, she was pulled back into the mirror. She struggled a bit, trying to get away, but Tim was too strong, he pulled her in. Inside the blackness, she looked out towards her living room, grabbed the edge of the mirror and tried to hold on, but she couldn't hold on for long. As she let go, the mirror tumbled backwards to the floor and shattered.

The next morning when her family came to check on her, they found nothing but melted piles of wax throughout the house and one broken mirror.

# THE WINNING PROP

It was going to be a glorious day for Ruben. The day he yearned for forever. A day he had plotted, planned and prepped since last Halloween. This year, he was sure to win the *Most Haunted House* contest. He was shooting for the *Scariest House* title. It wasn't the prize he cared about (oh boy!, two tickets to see the local production of Rocky Horror), what he really wanted was the satisfaction of finally beating his brother at something. For forty-six years, Lars has been the better one. Better grades, better job, better girlfriends, first to get married and the best looking. Ruben was constantly in his shadow. This was the year he was going to walk out from under it by taking the title of *Scariest House* away from his brother who won it the last few years in a row.

Halloween was always a favorite holiday of his, but for years he just put out a pathetic pumpkin on his tiny little house's steps. Then five years ago, the town started the Haunted House competition to boost tourism as they went for the title of the "New England town with the most Spirit(s)". Lars won the first year. It was that win that started Ruben's interest in the competition. Finally, something he could have a chance to beat his brother at. After his brother won, Ruben went out and bought half price decorations the day after Halloween and stored them till the next year. Neither of them won that following year, resulting in both of them spending three grand each buying up decorations and lights for future use. Due to a faulty wire that made his electric chair man prop not work, Ruben lost the next year as well. Then last year, just when he thought he had it in the bag, he lost because his brother had secretly rigged a flying bat to pop out and scare the judges. It was that bat that won it, so he was told.

That is why this year, instead of just decorating the front yard, Ruben went all out. Not only were there decorations, he turned his yard and garage into a haunted house experience that matched the likes of professional haunted houses. At least he liked to think so. The farthest anyone had taken the competition (his brother of course), was to turn their garage into a mini-haunted house. Ruben was taking it further. He bought over sixty tarps and dozens of pipes to make a haunted tunnel. It started in the front yard, wrapped around to the back of the house and led into the garage's backdoor. Through the tunnel he rigged dozens of strobe lights, smoke machines and various creepy decorations, even motion triggered zombies that popped out and made noise when you walked by it. He even set up a camera system so he could monitor when people were coming in, especially the judges.

Of course when they entered the garage... that was the best part, the finale! It took him days to cover the walls with black tarps, rig the strobes, set up the sacrificial alter and make it look creepy. Ruben was to play the role of a satanic priest. When people entered the room they would see him standing behind the altar in a costume he designed himself. Smoke would cover the ground and a giant fake body would lay on the altar. He would mumble some gibberish and swing down a giant knife into the chest of the dummy sending blood spraying in the air (he rigged a pump that he controlled with his foot to shoot the blood out). At that exact second he would trigger the speakers, loud booming screams and the devil's voice

167

would ring out over the scared visitors telling them all that Satan had risen and would take their souls. Three seconds later a hole in the floor would open up, spilling red light on the crowd as a giant hand reached out to bring them all down to Hell (this prop cost him a fortune and almost two months to get just right). At that point, Ruben would laugh and yell that all who want to be saved must leave now through the side door that he would open by pulling a string. Once outside there would be a giant bowl of candy for them. It was brilliant, complicated, needing hours of practice and tweaking of the machines, but all worth it, if he won.

As the sun started to set on Halloween night, Ruben cracked open the bags of candy, poured them into the massive bowl and hummed to himself. In a mere hour the fun would begin and he would be on his way to winning first place. Life was good, for once. In a matter of minutes he had on his black priest suit, cape and satanic medallion necklace he bought on EBay. With a pat of powder and a bit of black makeup under his eyes, he was ready. Excitement flowed through him. The last time he was this excited he was ten and it was Christmas morning. Of course Santa gave the present *he* wanted to Lars.

With minutes left, Ruben did his last walk through. He checked every prop, light, machine and inch of the wall to make sure no outside light came in. It was all beyond perfect. Satisfied, he ran to the front, put up the *Not Welcome* sign and ran to his position to await the first visitors. It was not a long wait at that. Within five minutes he could hear screams and giggles as people entered into his award winning (hopefully) display. Peeking at the monitors he saw that it was teens. He hated teens, they were always tough to scare and annoying. Then he realized it would be good practice, scaring them meant he could scare the judges.

As the door opened to let in his first victims, teens or not, he almost cried with excitement.

"Ahhhhhhh! More souls to send to Hell! Is that what you wish for?" Ruben screamed in his best theatrical scary voice. It was a small group of three, one teen boy acted tough and two girls clutched to him like he was a life raft.

"Musta, krakum, upulah, TEGUM!" He mumbled raising the knife high and swinging it down. Having found that the plastic knifes bent too easily and didn't shine good enough, he was using a real eight-inch chef's knife. He was only plunging it into latex anyway, so it was safe. *Splurk*, the knife hit, the blood spurted and the sound effects started to boom, it was beautiful, he had to do his best to not smile.

"Ewwww! Gross." One of the girls cried out.

"What is taking Nick so long, he should have caught up to us by now?" The other girl cried out grabbing on to her friends, obviously needing her boyfriend to keep her protected. The trap door opened up, the hand started to reach out and they all scooted back a bit.

"All of you who want to be saved, leave now…leave…or be forever in HELL!" The trio raced for the door, the boy laughing, saying something about how his buddy was on his own. With the door shut Ruben let out a hoot of success, then quickly ducked under the table to check the monitors for more people. A slim teen wearing an orange pumpkin shirt was heading for the door, their friend, Ruben assumed. Though the sign to wait was lit, the kid tried the door handle, shouldered it and got it to swing open before Ruben was ready. There was a tearing, snapping, pop sound. Ruben was furious. The kid had just broken the remote control mechanism on the door that opened it, and, he was in before the hand had reset. The kid was ruining everything.

"You broke my damn door kid, just get the hell out of here." He pointed to the door. The kid laughed and started a light jog towards the door. Not seeing the giant red hand, his foot caught on the claw, sending him sprawling face first to the floor. With the darkness and fog Ruben couldn't see how bad he hit, but heard a wet smack. Annoyed, he waited a few seconds for the kid to get up, but he didn't. Grabbing the emergency flashlight from under the counter he grudgingly went to the kid. Rolling him over he gasped at the sight. The kid's nose was flat to his face, two teeth protruded out of his upper lip and blood was dripping everywhere.
"Wake up kid, wake up!" Ruben yelled before lowering his head to hear if the kid could speak, there was a low gurgling sound, but nothing else.

With panic setting in he got up and shot to the door to get the kid's friends and call the police. As his hand hit the handle the electric *ding* told him more people had entered the tunnel. *What if it was the judges?* Racing to the monitor he almost fainted as he saw a small group holding clipboards entering. It meant he had three minutes exactly till they reached this room. If he left the garage and called the police now, it would be all over with, he'd lose, probably even get a lawsuit. All this money and time would be for nothing. Back at the monitor he switched the camera to the front of the house. The three teens were still there, the boy looked to be arguing about leaving.

"Go, that's right, just go, your friend never came in here." Seeing the kid walk away and the two girls reluctantly follow he realized that maybe this accident was a gift. A gift that could help him win.

Racing to the back door, he was thankful that the wire had merely popped of its wheel and not broken like he thought, an easy fix. With the help of a screwdriver, he had the wire back on in a second. Then it was off to his altar. Lifting up the fake body he laid it next to the altar, tipped its head forward and laughed at how good it looked, he should have thought about having more bodies around before. The hard part of lifting the kid up and placing him on the altar came next. It took several heaves and a few pulled muscles in his back, but he got the kid, who was thankfully skinny, on the altar. Less than a minute left. He raced to the door, looked at the body lying there and made sure it didn't look *too* real. Thankfully with the lights and smoke it could pass as realistic, but not too real, besides who would think a real body was lying in a thing like this? To be safe he swung the kid's head away from where the judges would be standing. It was time.

Trembling, but ready, the door swung open, he said his lines, doing his best to not look at the judges faces and raised his knife high in the air. He could hear a few gasps and murmurs of *how realistic!* Then, to his surprise, the kid raised his arm out for help. Ruben had planned to bring the knife down next to the body, but now that the kid was moving he panicked as he swung the knife down. The blade plunged in the dead center of the kid's chest. The boy lurched forward, blood shot out of his chest and sprayed out of his mouth before he fell back and convulsed on the table. Ruben couldn't help but look at the judges whose faces had gone slack with shock. Hitting the button for the floor, he prayed they thought it was just an amazing animatronics doll.

"Leave…. LEAVE NOW!" Hesitantly, hey left. Ruben fell to his knees, gasped for air and then laughed as he saw the blood and a chunk of flesh on his knife. As long as they didn't think it was real, he knew he'd win the contest.

Over and over again that night, Ruben brought the knife down on the boy until the hole in his chest was so large he had to stab him in the stomach. Every person looked scared, but no one thought it was a real body. A bit before eleven one last group of teens went through, laughed at how fake the blood looked and disappeared out the door. At the end of the night he started to think of ways to get rid of the boy before anyone came sniffing around. As he started to wrap the legs in trash bags the house phone rang, the caller ID said it was his brother.

"Happy Halloween Bro." Ruben said with tension building in his stomach.

"Congratulations… you won. Don't know how you beat me, especially with my set up this year, but you did it. Mind if I stop by and check it out in a few minutes?" Ruben could feel the tear streak down his face, smudging his makeup. He won…*he* won.

"Sure. Sure come by!" Hanging up the phone he screamed, jumped up and down and cheered before kissing the boy's forehead. As his lips left the cold skin he realized his brother would take more time in there than everyone else, he would see the body was real. Grabbing the kid's legs he pulled the body off the table, it smacked the ground with a crunch and splat, part of his shirt fell off of him, having been torn open in so many places. It took a lot of effort and sweat, but he was able to pull the body out of the garage and behind the shed in the backyard just as he saw his brother pull up. Racing like a maniac he put the fake body back in place, touched up his makeup and shouted out the door for his brother to go in the main entrance.

Five minutes later, the two were chatting and Ruben was gloating.

"I thought the body on the altar would look more realistic, that is all people talked about. Judges were amazed by it. Hmmm. I'm proud of you though, bro." It was the sentence he always wanted to hear. It was like music to his ears. Ruben was so elated that he didn't realize two police officers had entered the tunnel until they were banging on the door.

"Oh…can I help you two or were you just going through for fun? Because if you were, I'll have to reset everything."

"Actually, we're looking for a kid. He disappeared somewhere around your house about five hours ago. Here's his picture, recognize him?" With a huge gulp, Ruben laughed and said he saw a lot of kids that night and couldn't be sure.

"Well if you think of…" The officer was cut off as the other one nudged him, walked over in front of the altar and picked up a piece of cloth.

"Didn't they say he was wearing an orange pumpkin shirt?" The officer held up the orange cloth smeared with blood. Ruben rubbed his face, smudging the makeup more.

"That's…it could be…" he couldn't even get the sentence out. Within ten minutes they had found the body and put cuffs on him. As he was being walked to the squad car he cried to his brother.

"They won't take away the title will they? There is no rule saying we couldn't use real props, right? I still won, I beat you, damn it! I won! I won…."

# JACK RABBIT

"There he goes again." Mitch sighed. Julie rolled over to face him with a sigh of her own. At first, the new neighbor's noise turned them both on a bit; they even made love after being awoken by it the first time. The thought of another couple having sex a mere ten feet above them was exciting. A dash of spice their routine sex life needed. It was a different story now.

For over a month they had been awoken almost every night between 11:30 p.m. and 1:00 a.m.. The same thing every night. *Squeak, squeak, squeak, squeak, squeak.* The damn noisiest bed in the world as Mitch liked to call it, and it was right above their bed in the third floor apartment. After that first night of making love to the noise they just sat and listened to the repetitive squeaking. The second night they giggled at how the man never took a break and probably didn't even change positions as there was never a pause long enough for him to do so.

"He's like a jack hammer! Non-stop. I feel bad for that poor woman. Good god!" Julie laughed as they both stared at the ceiling as if they looked hard enough they'd be able to see through it. The third and fourth night it started to lose its entertainment value and another conversation about the man started.

"I think he is having sex with a blow up doll." Mitch said after the first ten minutes of squeaking.

"Think about it, it makes sense. I don't think many women would put up with that non-stop pounding for so long. And when he finishes, I only hear one person get up and go to the bathroom. I never hear other footsteps up there." Julie contemplated what Mitch had just said.

"Maybe she doesn't weigh enough to make noise when she walks. Then again, you could be right. It would explain a lot." After the first month a decision was made. He was having a sex with a blow up doll. They had no doubt in their minds and Mitch was still curious about this man. He lived right above them, yet he had never seen him.

Working from home as a website designer Mitch often got bored during the day and looked for distractions, like spying on his neighbors in the apartment complex. Nothing serious, he was just a curious man who liked to watch people as they walked through the courtyard. What he enjoyed most was trying to figure out who lived where. Though they had lived there for over a year, they really hadn't met any of their neighbors. And it wasn't for lack of trying.

One day while trying to put a crawl on a website for an author, Mitch heard the man upstairs getting ready to leave. The door slammed and he could hear him on the steps. Without hesitating Mitch jumped up, ran through the living room, tripped on a pair of sneakers by the door but made it in time to look through the peephole to get his first view of the man that Julie had recently nicknamed, *The Jack Rabbit*. To his disappointment, the man looked normal. He was a regular guy in his mid-thirties wearing a black polo with a yellow logo on the right breast. It was his first clue; he worked for a cell phone company.

That night Mitch excitedly told Julie this information. She didn't seem to care nearly as much as he did. She seemed to lose interest in the man when they came to the conclusion that there wasn't an actual couple having sex upstairs. The only thing she cared about now was getting him to stop, or at least oil his bed frame. She got up at six every morning and she went to bed at ten. So when the squeaking started it woke her up right about the time she had just fallen asleep, every night. That missing hour of sleep was starting to wear on her nerves.

"That's great honey. You saw the man. How about now you go upstairs, knock on his door and ask him to fuck his doll a bit softer or maybe in the living room... so I can get some sleep." Mitch contemplated her response for a minute, it would be exciting to see inside of his apartment, to see what it was like, but that would require confronting him. It was out of the question.

"Why don't we leave a note on the door?" Mitch suggested. Julie rolled her eyes and went to the bathroom to get ready for bed.

"Well it would be a bit awkward telling a man to have quieter sex! A note should do the trick? No?" Mitch questioned. Brushing her teeth, Julie gave a gurgled response.

"Yeah, and why don't you leave a bottle of WD-40 with the note?" She spit and continued her response.

"Instead, why don't you just sneak into his place while he is gone and oil the bed. That way you wouldn't have to confront him at all." With that Mitch realized Julie was in no mood to mess with, he receded his ground and went to bed to read. That night when the squeaking started Julie ignored it with a pillow over her head, Mitch just stared at the ceiling imagining Julie's suggestion; sneaking in.

The next day, when he should have been working, Mitch spent hours researching how to pick locks on the Internet. After getting a firm grasp of the technique, he went about trying it out on his own door. Making sure that no one was around first, he took his keys with him, locked the door behind him and went about trying to get in without the keys. Using a few household items he already had, Mitch successfully picked his own lock…two days later on the forty-seventh try. Another four days later he was a master at it. He knew without a doubt that he could get into the apartment upstairs, mostly because it was a carbon copy of his place. The question was, did he actually have the balls to do it. Part of him knew he never would, yet the other part of him was more excited than it had been in years at the aspect of doing something…adventurous. Maybe never leaving the apartment and sitting behind his computer all day was getting to him.

After gaining confidence in his lock picking skills Mitch listened for hours on end to the man upstairs. Sometimes he sat for three hours without hearing a peep. Day after day he listened intently, until he finally learned the man's routine. Up at nine, shower, TV for an hour. Then he would leave about ten minutes before eleven for work which he didn't return from until eight at night. That meant he had about a six-hour window to get in the apartment and look around, finally get to see the doll he was fucking, maybe oil the bed, then get back downstairs. Plenty of time.

A few days passed. Mitch resumed his normal work, but found himself thinking about going upstairs more and more. Each day after the Jack Rabbit would leave, he would sit staring at the ceiling, knowing no one was up there. No one would see him breaking in. The apartment was on the third floor, there were only three other apartments, two of which were vacant at the moment and the fourth one's tenant was a huge five-hundred pound man who hasn't left his apartment in years. The chances of getting caught were slim to none, although that didn't make it any less nerve-racking.

177

Instead of fulfilling his silly fantasy, he sat day in and day out in front of his computer, trying to work, yet dying to build up the courage he needed to make the journey.

It was three days later when Julie was woken up at quarter to one from the squeaking. She got so annoyed she almost ran up the stairs and pounded on the door at that very moment.

"I can't take it anymore! Maybe I'll complain to the office? They could do something, right?" Mitch took this as the last bit of fuel he needed, he had to be a man, to take a risk for once in his life. To be the knight in shining armor who killed the dragon for his fair maiden. Only this dragon was a bed that needed some oiling.

"I'll take care of it, I promise, tomorrow." Julie grumbled something about how it would never happen and went back to sleep. Mitch stared at the ceiling, knowing the next day he would be up there. He could barely sleep he was so excited.

The next day Mitch kissed Julie goodbye like always and sat behind his desk to "work". The plan was to wait until one. That way the Rabbit would be gone for two hours and most people would be heading back to work after lunch. That gave him four hours to sit, plan, wait and be nervous. The plan was to leave his apartment door unlocked, that way he could rush down and enter quickly if need be. Secondly he would wear a disguise. A hooded jacket, sunglasses and baseball cap, might be a bit suspicious, but at least if he had to run away from the apartment he wouldn't be recognized, then he could ditch the outer layer in the dumpster area in back and walk up the stairs to his apartment like nothing had happened. It would work perfectly.

While waiting, he prepared the items he would need. The tools to pick the lock, yellow rubber dish gloves to conceal his fingerprints and a small can of WD-

40 to oil the bedsprings with. He laid them all out on the kitchen counter, put his outfit on and still had two hours to wait. Two hours that ticked by like days.

Finally it was time. Two minutes before one, Mitch looked out of every window in his apartment, there was no one around. Slipping out of his door he double-checked that it was left open. Then, trembling like he was about to ask a girl out for the first time, he made his way up the stairs. There was a small landing half way up there he once again looked around, no one. At the top of the stairs he walked past the door, almost losing his nerve. Then he came back, looked at it to make sure there was nothing suspicious about it and tried the handle. Locked. Dropping to his knees he pulled out the thin metal tools and went about working the bottom lock first. Within seconds it sprung loose. He was sweating profusely and felt like he had to vomit as he turned the knob. It had worked; next he had to work on the deadbolt, much harder than the simple handle lock. This one took a few tries, his hands were shaking a bit too much to get the right angle, but finally on the fifth try it popped loose.

Mitch stood up, pocketed the tools and looked at the door as if it were the gate to Hell. Was he really going to do this? Commit a felony? Though was it a felony if you just oiled a bed frame? Mitch thought of turning back, of taking off his yellow dish gloves and running to the safety of his own apartment, then he thought of how he would have nothing to do, but sit and work. This was the most excitement he had in years, he had to push forward. With that, Mitch turned the handle and pushed the door open.

The layout inside was just as he expected, a carbon copy his place. Yet it looked nothing like theirs at all. Instead of the bright, warm colors and chic interior design that Julie was so proud of, there was almost nothing. A television sitting on the box it came in, an old beat up recliner in front of it. The kitchen to the left had nothing on the counters. Looking around Mitch realized he had left the door open and frantically shut it behind him, a bit too loud. He took a few seconds to catch his breath and went back to observing the apartment. Off to the right where the living room lead into what was his office was nothing but a bunch of moving boxes, un-opened. Mitch stepped as lightly as he could, trying not to make a sound, until he realized that it was his apartment downstairs and no one would hear him walking. He chuckled to himself and went to the fridge to see what the man ate. Opening it up he wasn't surprised to see boxes of takeout food, a few beers and nothing else. As he shut the door he realized he was here for a reason, and snooping was not it. Besides, the longer he was there, the higher his chances of getting caught.

Getting back on track, Mitch left the kitchen and made a beeline for the bedroom, though he couldn't help but peek into the bathroom on the way. There was nothing much in it either, a clear shower curtain, a few dirty towels and what looked like a bunch of fruit punch stains on the wall. Mitch shrugged to himself and stepped towards the bedroom. One foot in, he jumped a mile and ran for the front door in a panic. As he grasped the handle he started to laugh hysterically. What he saw in the bedroom wasn't a woman under the blankets. It had to be the blow up doll! Gaining his composure, he couldn't believe Julie was right, the man actually bangs and sleeps next to a blow up doll!

With a bounce in his step he made his way back to the bedroom door and looked in. This time he took in the whole room. The carpet had juice stains all over it and there was clothing and food wrappers everywhere. The bed was just a full size mattress sitting on an old frame which explained the squeaking. Though the doll was under the blankets with just a tuft of hair sticking out, it looked real. Mitch started to wonder if this slob spent all his money on one of those Real Dolls, those ones that cost five-thousand bucks, but were so "life like" they were worth the cost, he always wondered what they felt like.

Mitch wanted to look at the doll, but decided to save it for the last thing. Better oil the frame first. He dropped to his knee next to the bed and pulled out the small can. Lifting up the sheets he was shocked to see an array of weapons, it instantly made him nervous of getting caught. A man with seven different knifes and three guns under his bed probably didn't take too kindly to strangers breaking into his apartment. He took a deep breath and sprayed the liquid on all the hinges he could see, got up went to the other side and repeated the process. The room smelled a bit like oil, he only hoped that it would go away before the Rabbit got back.

Finished and proud of himself, Mitch stood up puffed up his chest and looked around the room. He couldn't believe he actually did it. He looked at the floor and pictured his bedroom below, *he was actually up here*. Mitch did his best to remember every detail of the room, that way he could remember it when he stared at the ceiling at night. The last thing he had to do, the thing he was thrilled about, was to look at the doll. Hell, if it was as real as the ad made it out to be, maybe he'd have to try it, then again, who knew how often the guy cleaned it.

Mitch reached out and touched the hair sticking out from the blanket, it was amazingly real. Didn't they use horsehair on dolls? This seemed much more real, then again, for five grand, it should. Then Mitch grabbed the crusty white sheet and pulled it back to get a look at the doll's face. He was expecting to see a hot looking, yet creepy expression frozen with a blowjob mouth gapped

181

open. The creepy part was right, only the expression was horror and the skin wasn't smooth and taught, it was dried and wrinkled with veins of purple and green showing through. And the eyes, they were gone, leaving crusty holes, one of which was filled with a drying creamy liquid. It was about the same time that he realized what the liquid in the empty eye socket was that he also realized that this wasn't a doll… it was a dead body.

Mitch jumped back so fast and hard he slammed into the wall, popping a small hole in the sheetrock with his elbow. At the same time his hand, frozen shut on the sheet, pulled the cover off the corpse, revealing the full body. The body was nude, covered only in bulbous bruises, gray and yellow veins and half a dozen holes cut out of her stomach, neck, leg and her right breast. She was a small girl; maybe five feet tall, if it weren't for the large, shriveling fake breasts, Mitch would have thought she was a child. After twenty seconds of shock, the vomit came as he noticed the stains on the sheets. Around the entire body were yellow, brown and gray blotches from where her body was leaking fluids of rot.

With his hand over his mouth he was able to make it out of the room before vomiting fully. Half of it landed in the bathroom sink, the other half on the floor. After a few heaves he took a sobbing deep breath and wretched at the smell of his own vomit. Making him wonder why the body didn't smell, or did his shock just block his senses? In a panic, Mitch started to clean up his puke with a towel that was on the floor, a towel he quickly noticed was crunchy and stained with that fruit punch color as well. He threw it aside falling backwards on his ass in the doorway. What the hell should he do? First things first, he had to get the hell out of the apartment.

Getting over his fear of the crunchy towel he picked it back up and cleaned the rest of his vomit with it.

Then he took the towel and hid it under the sink behind the plumbing, hoping the Rabbit wouldn't find it for a while at least. He was about to leave when he realized he had left the body uncovered. He'd have to go back in and cover her up. He knew that no matter what he did, the image of that mangled body would be stuck in his mind forever, seeing it one more time wouldn't kill him, as horrible as it is.

Standing in the doorway he couldn't help but stare at the seeping, rotting body. He and Julie made love to the sounds of the Rabbit having sex with, with a corpse? For weeks he had been listening to the squeaking, getting turned on by it, wanting nothing more than to watch what was going on and the whole time that sick bastard was sticking his dick into cut out holes on a dead woman… the thought almost made him vomit again. Breathing through his mouth he shut his eyes, counted to three and walked across the room. All he had to do was pull the bed sheet up. He could do it.

At the foot of the bed he couldn't help but wonder who the girl was. Did he see her picture on the local news: *Missing girl, have you seen me?* Ignoring the flood of thoughts that were rising in his brain he grabbed the sheet, muttered, sorry, and pulled it back up. Then he turned to the wall, he gasped at how noticeable the hole was, but what could he do? He had no choice but to leave it.

More than ready to leave, Mitch turned to the door and started to walk on his weak legs when he noticed a cord coming out of the closet door. Every sense in him told him to just keep walking, to get the hell out. Yet a tiny part of him said, *look. What if there was another victim, alive in the closet?* Judging by the deterioration of the corpse on the bed, the odds of that were tiny, but he couldn't help but take a look. Again, it was the same as their apartment, a walk in closet. He flicked on the light switch outside of the door and tried the handle; it stuck a bit, but then gave. Inside, Mitch saw another view that would be forever burned into his memory. There were almost no clothes hanging, the only thing hanging from hooks were two female heads, much more deteriorated than the body on the bed. Again both eyes were gone, but they weren't that far, they were in a jar on the shelf, along with what looked like to be a dozen eyes all staring at him, asking for help. Mitch was numb. When he saw the pair of breasts nailed to the far wall, his mind starting to shut down. Looking below the shriveled breasts he saw a computer monitor set up on a make shift desk that had a milk crate for a seat. On the screen he couldn't believe what he saw. It was a live image of his bedroom.

Doing his best to ignore the heads that brushed his shoulders as he walked to the computer he used the mouse to click around. Seven cameras. One in his bathroom, one in the bedroom, one on the door to the Rabbit's apartment, one in the guy's bedroom, one in the bathroom, one to the gate entrance and one at the road. Then on the bottom of the screen he noticed the tiny blinking light…*Sending Live Feed.* Seeing the icon immediately snapped Mitch back into reality. The bastard might live like a slob and kill women, but he wasn't stupid. He had the place wired to know if the cops ever showed up. He'd been watching this whole time. Mitch looked at his watch, it was twenty-three minutes after one. He'd been in the apartment for over twenty minutes. That is plenty of time for the Rabbit to get back and… do God knows what to him.

Not caring about hiding his presence any more, Mitch grabbed a flash drive stick out of the computer, hoping it had evidence, then snagged the wires to the computer and ripped them out. Then he was off and running through the apartment, out the door, down the stairs and into his own place. Slamming the door he locked all three locks and leaned against it, his face being cooled by the cold of the door, a slow sob of tears running down his face cooled him down even more. He was safe…safe.

"Hey Neighbor!"

Mitch could feel all the blood in his body run cold. It was as if gravity was suddenly pulling on him harder than ever before. He didn't want to turn around, to face the reality of what was happening. Why was he stupid enough to go upstairs? Why did he leave his door unlocked when he went up there?

"It's about time we met, don't you think?" The voice sounded a bit closer, for fear of getting stabbed in the back Mitch spun around keeping his back against the door. The Jack Rabbit was sitting at the breakfast bar, only six feet away. Not nearly far enough to give him time to get out the door and run. He started to curse himself for not bringing a weapon to this mission.

"The name is Paul, but I guess you can call me Rabbit. And yours?" The man put out his hand, his knuckles where worn and red as if he punched things on a regular basis. Mitch didn't offer a hand; he stayed right where he was trying to figure out something he could do. The man didn't look to be in great shape, but he had experience with guns and knives and probably had been in a lot of fights. Mitch had none of that, though he was in shape.

"It's alright, I know your name is Mitch, and your girl…. Julie. Sweet body on her. Wouldn't mind having a new play toy…as you saw mine is getting a bit…used I guess you can say." The man fidgeted in his chair making Mitch jump a bit. The Rabbit chuckled at this.

"Seems we got ourselves a bit of a situation here. You know if you had the balls to just ask me to be quieter upstairs, we wouldn't be sitting here now. I'm guessing by now you figured out that I have your place wired. I'd like to say for safety reasons, but I get off on watching people too. Ever just watch someone when they didn't know anyone could see them Mitch?" Mitch was listening, but he looked around the room trying to figure a way out, as if he didn't know every item in the place already.

"It's thrilling to just watch people...be. Or to watch a couples daily sex routine, or to watch how someone showers. By the way, did you know Julie masturbates almost every time after you have sex? Either when you go to the bathroom to wash up, or when she goes to take a "shower" afterwards. Guess you don't satisfy her as much as she says. See those are the things you learn by watching." Mitch finally opened his mouth.

"What are you going to do to me?" The man smiled, got up and walked to the recliner in the living room and sat. It was still not far enough away for Mitch to make a break for it.

"You know, I was a bit offended at the nickname you and Julie first gave me, but now. I kind of like it. The Jack Rabbit! Makes me sound...fast, slick. Truthfully it is fitting. I have been getting away with my hobby for years. Can't let you fuck that up, now can I?" Mitch swallowed hard trying to moisten his rapidly drying throat. He started to curse himself in his head about how much of a wuss he was. First he couldn't even knock on someone's door to tell him to be quiet. Now he can barely speak to even save his own life. What kind of man was he?

"I don't get much pleasure out of killing men. But I do it when I have to survive. In a way this might work out well. You guys never have visitors, so no one will really know you're gone for a while. I could whack you now, wait for Julie and make her my new toy for a few days. Then I'll just head off to the next location." Mitch could tell he was getting a kick out of terrifying him. He was merely batting him around like a cat with a mouse, playing with it before they sink their teeth in.

Mitch knew that if he wanted to live he was going to have to fight his way out of this, somehow. Though he didn't know if he could get the courage up to do it, he'd rather die fighting. Most of all, he had to somehow protect Julie, give her a warning to not come home. If only he could get his cell phone. He could see it sitting on the desk ten feet behind the Rabbit. The Rabbit caught his gaze and swiveled the chair around to see what he was looking at. This was the added seconds Mitch needed. If he raced out now, he might make it.

Mitch spun around, flipped the deadbolt to unlock and turned the handle. As he pulled the door open he heard the springs on the recliner release as The Rabbit got up. With the door open he ran as fast as he could out the door to the stairs. At the top of the stairs he felt hands on his back, only they weren't pulling him backwards, they were pushing him forward. A split second later...everything went black as his face hit the edge of the concrete stair.

When Mitch woke up he realized he was in his own bed, the sun was setting. Was it a dream? When he went to get up, but couldn't because of the ropes that tied him down, he realized it wasn't. The pain was horrible, every limb was numb, his face pounded. He tried to scream out in agony but realized that his jaw wouldn't move because it was broken. A few seconds later he realized that his left wrist, nose and right leg were also broken. The concrete stairs definitely did a number on him, unless The Rabbit did a bit more to ensure he didn't move. But why was he even keeping him alive?

Mitch did his best to crane his neck to see the clock, it was just about five. Julie would be home in a matter of twenty minutes. Terrified of what would happen to her, Mitch gurgled the loudest he could to get someone, anyone's attention. The Rabbit came into the room with a big smile.

"Thought you'd never wake up pal!" He jumped on the bed, on Julie's side, and laughed at the pain the bounce caused in Mitch.

"Tried to run on me...you forgot, I'm quick as a Rabbit, remember?" Another sick giggle. Mitch closed his eyes desperately wanting to be able to speak clearly.

"Listen. You are alive for one reason and one reason only. I need the pin number for your ATM card. If you are making me run, you're going to have to finance it. I looked through your computer and files, doesn't look like you wrote it down. So I'll make you a deal, tell me it and I'll kill you quickly, don't and I'll make you watch me cut your girl's eye out and cum inside the empty socket while she is still alive. Got it?"

Mitch started to cry. He could hear the man next to him lay back and get comfortable.

"You better hurry, Julie will be home in a few minutes. I can't wait too... Christ her tits are huge, love that." Mitch tried to talk, but started coughing instead, spitting up a glob of blood and mucus onto his own chin. Clearing his throat a bit he grunted a few times to show he couldn't speak.

"Tell you what, I'll get you a pen and paper, let you write it down, it'll be easier for me to remember." As the man left the room Mitch stared at the ceiling. It looked different now, before it used to tempt him, mystify his thoughts. Now, now it terrified him.

The Rabbit came back in, loosened Mitch's good arm, slapped a pen in his hand a placed the pad under it. Mitch didn't know what to do. Dying without having to see Julie suffer would be best, but if he died now, he wouldn't be able to do anything to save her. Without even realizing it, his hand wrote *Fuck you* in a barely legible scratch. The Rabbit chuckled, then out of nowhere he pulled a small butterfly knife out, jabbed it in Mitch's leg and started sawing a circle. Mitch screamed as loud as he could, it did nothing to stop the pain, the blade was in so deep it was hitting the bone. After almost a full minute The Rabbit had cut a full two-inch round circle of meat out of his leg, which was now bleeding profusely. The man held up the chunk full of skin, fat, muscle and other inner workings in the air as it dripped deep red blood onto the white sheets. The man looked at it for a few seconds as Mitch did the best he could to not pass out. Then he quickly inserted the chunk of meat into Mitch's mouth, pushed up his broken jaw and made Mitch chew it over and over again. Mitch nearly choked to death on his own leg meat. He was only saved by the vomit that came up, clearing his mouth out.

"Oh how I'm going to make her suffer Mitch. And as you watch every tear stream down her face…you'll know it was because of you." With that he spit on Mitch and left the room. Mitch passed out…only for a minute though.

Julie had called Mitch several times before leaving work. Each time he hadn't answered. That was not normal for Mitch. If he didn't answer he would call back seconds later. It has been two hours since she first called him. She was a bit worried and on her way home she had a horrible feeling of dread. One of those "a mother always knows" feelings, even though she wasn't a mother…just yet. She only found out she was pregnant three weeks ago. It was why she had been so irritable, she was scared to tell anyone for she didn't even know if she was going to keep it herself or not.

As she went up the stairs to the door she noticed what looked to be specs of blood on the steps, her heart sank. *Something was not right.* When she tried the door handle and it wasn't locked she knew something was horribly wrong. In one hand she readied her mace that Mitch made her carry on her evening walks alone, in the other hand she grabbed her cell phone ready to call for help. Then she pushed the door open. Everything looked normal, except there was no sign of Mitch and there again were those drops, more in here than outside. Leaving the door open she walked in like a scared cat ready to jump backwards. She yelled Mitch's name twice, she thought she heard something from the bedroom but wasn't sure.

Looking down at her phone she punched in 911 and readied her finger above the send button. As she walked by the kitchen she took a deep breath. For some reason she wanted to enjoy this last second, for instinctively she knew everything in her life would change after this. And she was right. When she reached the bathroom a man pounced on her. The second she was hit she pushed the send button on the phone, or so she hoped, as it flew out of her hand and skidded across the carpet. With the other hand she was able to hold onto the mace. On the ground the man had her pinned pretty well, but she was tough, and struggled enough to keep him from getting a full grip on her.

Wriggling the hand with the mace free she was able to spray it, the only problem was his face was only inches from hers. She took a solid blast of it as well. The evil, painful scent filled her nose, sending daggers into her lungs and razor blades into her eyes. She only hoped the pain was just as intense for him. Apparently it was, he rolled off of her screaming.

Mitch lay on the bed crying, trying his best to scream and fidget free. Neither were of much success.

He could only imagine what was going on out there. Julie wasn't that strong, though she was in shape. Could she fight him off enough to save herself? Never had he felt so helpless.

Staring at the ceiling he thought of the dozens of weapons under the bed above him, only feet away. He wished he had taken one when he realized he had his own weapon inches from him. A weapon he had never used, yet always had ready in case of an emergency. Ever since he moved out of his parent's house at the age of twenty, he kept an old plastic billy club next to his bed...just in case. The thought of the weapon excited him for a minute then he realized it would do him no good in this state.

Crackling moans and yells is all Mitch heard outside the door. Then seconds later Julie stumbled into the room like a blind person. It took Mitch a few seconds to realize it was with good reason. She had used her mace, the mace he bought her! He tried to scream, *lock the door* to her, but it came out as "Ooar". It was enough to get his point across. With her eyes shut she felt for the door, swung it shut and locked the flimsy handle lock, that couldn't keep out a four year old for more than a few minutes. Mitch then screamed "urah". Julie was good at interpreting him and hurried over to his side of the bed. Without even having to tell her, she knew enough to grab the bottle of eye drops he kept next to the bed for his dry eyes.

Instead of instilling the usual one to two drops she squeezed half the bottle into one of her eyes and the other half in the other. Though it didn't do much, it still felt amazing and it enabled her to see a bit clearer. Seeing Mitch tied to the bed she quickly went about untying him. Luckily for her, the man wasn't any good at knots, the ties were tied like shoelaces enabling her to just pull one thread at a time to loosen him. Once untied, Mitch still wasn't too mobile, but at least he could move a bit. "Ulie ub, Ulie ub!" Mitch gurgled. This translation took a few seconds longer but Julie finally understood it, dropped to her knees next to the bed and found the dust encrusted club. It was no match for a gun or a knife, but it would definitely help them.

Julie held the club in front of her like it was a flash light, clearly not ready or knowing how to use it. Mitch struggled but managed to get up and stand on one foot. Outside the door they could hear the water in the bathroom. The Rabbit must have been washing his face as well.

"I got him with the mace. My cell is out there though, I think I dialed 911, it might have not gotten through. What the hell should we do?" For the first time Mitch wished he had listened to his mother and gotten a "land line" in case of an "emergency", they never did think an emergency would occur.

An idea snapped into Mitch's head, though he didn't know how to communicate or execute it. Just like in the movies they had to barricade themselves in the room. Their dresser was over six feet long and four feet high, though he had no clue if they could move it on their own, especially in this state. Using his hands he pointed to the dresser and then the door. Julie immediately knew what he meant and went about trying to shove it. Amazingly she was able to move it an inch on her own. Mitch hobbled over to her with his jaw flapping freely from his head. Using his one good leg and arm he helped push. It took a few minutes but they were able to get it in front of the door. With their barricade in place he tried to smile, but then realized, The Rabbit wasn't trying to get in, there wasn't even noise out there. Had he left? Was he fleeing? Or was it a trick to get them to look to see if he was out there? It didn't matter; their next task would be to get them help. Mitch pointed to the window, motioned for Julie to open it then put his hand next to his face showing her to yell for help.

Julie slid the window open with ease and immediately stuck her head out to scream. And scream she did. The loudest and hardest she had ever screamed in her life. *Help*, over and over again. She knew a lot of people had to be home and hearing her, she just hoped that someone would call the cops and they would rush their asses over. That's when she saw the man she had just sprayed in the face walking through the courtyard with a backpack. At her screams he turned back to her and sprinted at the window. Not sure what he was doing and feeling safe, locked up here she kept screaming. She was noticing a few people starting to stick their heads out their windows to see what was going on. When she looked back towards the man, it was too late. She saw the gun in his hand go off, leaving her no time to move out of the way.

Sitting on the edge of the bed Mitch heard the gun shot a split second before a chunk of Julie's scalp hit him in the face, followed by a wet splat of brain matter and blood. For a full thirty seconds he sat there in shock, not sure what had just happened as Julie fell lifeless, half hanging out the window. After realizing that his idea had gotten Julie killed, Mitch wanted to die, he was in so much pain physically and mentally that he didn't even care if the Rabbit got away. Revenge was nowhere in his mind now. Death was…and only death.

Mitch fell to the floor embraced Julie's leg and thought of how he could kill himself. His only idea was to get upstairs…grab a gun and shoot himself before the cops arrived. Only he knew moving the bureau alone would be impossible. Then he realized, if he pulled Julie inside he could fall out the window and land on the concrete...that should do it.

As he pulled back Julie he had to look at the back of her head, half of it was missing, chunks of gore stuck in the hair he used to smell every night before he went to bed. By the time he had her inside he could hear someone entering the apartment, the police, he had to hurry. As he placed a blanket over Julie he wanted nothing more than to roll her over and kiss her one last time, but he knew if he saw her face, dead, mutilated, that it would haunt him even beyond the grave. Instead he kissed her back gently a few times, then caressed the one dry part of her hair before telling her he was sorry and that he loved her.

By the time he was pulling himself to the window the cops were forcing their way into the bedroom. *Jesus that was fast.* Inch by inch they had the door open a bit more, just as he moved closer and closer to being able to throw himself out of the window. By the time he had hoisted himself up enough to drop he could see that an officer had gotten the door open. He knew he had to let go, though for some reason he hesitated...then he realized why. The officer...*was* The Rabbit. His eyes were puffy and red and his uniform was unkempt.

"Hey Fucko! You got one tough bitch you know that? Too bad I won't have time to bang her. I do have time to kill you before my buddies in blue get here though." It was then he realized that the apartment upstairs wasn't where he lived, it was his play den, a ruse to throw people off. He went through so much trouble he even changed into a fake work uniform each day to make people believe he worked for a phone company. It was perfect Mitch realized. If he had lived through this he would have told them that the man worked for a cell phone company, making them never suspect one of their own.

"Shocked are we?" The Rabbit said snapping Mitch out of his thinking. Then the officer tossed the can of mace at him, it was empty but he needed Mitch's prints on it to show that he had sprayed him in the line of duty, forcing him to use lethal force. Then all he had to do was plant some drugs and make it look as if it was a drug deal gone bad. Hell, when he had run off he even wore a hoodie with a red bandana tied to his arm. Witnesses would remember that, tell the police and they would instantly think it was one of the local gangs. He was going to get away with this, hell he could probably even keep the apartment upstairs, no one had a clue that it was involved in any of it.

Mitch couldn't hold himself in the window anymore and fell back to the floor, on top of the billy club that Julie had dropped. Using his good arm he grabbed it while the officer edged closer to him.

"Look, just grab the can of mace off the floor and we'll get this over with." The Rabbit said looking over his shoulder to make sure no one else was nearby. Mitch pulled out the Billy club and pointed it at the man like it was a gun. The Rabbit started laughing so hard he looked away from Mitch, giving him enough time to wiz it right at his head. His aim was off and for the better; it hit the gun with enough force to knock it from the killer's hand. As the Rabbit scrambled to pick it up, Mitch used everything he had to lift himself back up into the window, this time he did not hesitate, he let go and fell backwards, flipping in the air on the way down, he landed on his back on top of the small shrubs below. He could feel half a dozen branches that broke and stuck into his back, but other than that he was alive and still conscious. *Fuck.*

By this time half the complex was outside, three men ran over to his aid just as the Rabbit stuck his head out the window ready to shoot at him. The two caught

*Michael Gore*

each other's eye, Mitch dug into his pocket, against the good citizens' advice and pulled out the memory stick he had taken from upstairs. As he held it up the Rabbit instantly knew what it was, his eyes grew large and he started shooting down at them. Two of the witnesses took bullets first, collapsing on top of Mitch, keeping him safe when the other five bullets followed.

When The Rabbit reached the bottom of the stairs to retrieve the small plastic stick, his fellow officers were on the scene, all of whom had their guns pointed on him.

96

# ZOMBIES!!

It was the thirty-seventh time Charlie had watched *Dawn of the Dead*. He loved the movie, and the special effects Tom Savini did, sick shit. Though he had only watched it so many times because he didn't have cable and it was one of only three DVDs he owned. As he drank his seventh beer of the night he looked at his hands, he cut them up pretty bad while tilling the field earlier in the day. Without even looking up, he quoted the lines from the film. The guy's guts were about to be ripped out, that always creeped him out, no matter how many times he saw it. Not wanting to look, he finished off his beer and got up to get another one.

As he walked towards the fridge he thought about zombies. There was some major ass kicking in the movie, but most of the characters end up dead. He wouldn't, he'd live, he'd be the one left standing with the hot chick. He would blow away zombies left and right, hell he already had four shotguns to do it with and he had plenty of practice with shooting foxes that tried to get on his farm. He was a crack shot, hardly took him more than two shots to hit those bastards, and they moved a lot faster than the undead. Too bad zombies weren't real; blowing some heads off would be a hoot.

Opening the beer at the sink he took a long sip and looked out the window. He hated this time of year, stupid Fall Fair taking up the Montgomery's farm. A mile away in the distance he could see the glow off all the lights, the twinkling of the ferris wheel, the Scream Tower flashing bright and of course the countless food vendors. If he shut of the TV he could hear the hum of the crowd, the screams, music and other annoying sounds. Every year for two solid weeks he had to put up with cars accidentally turning down his driveway, thinking they were at the right place. They'd do a u-turn and mess up his grass. Then the trash from the fairgrounds would blow over onto his field, it'd take him a week to clean it up. Yet no matter how much he complained to the town council, they held it every year.

Chugging the beer at the sink he could hear the scene was over, he could go back, he was feeling a bit dizzy, but he grabbed another beer anyway. Just as he was about to crack it open, there was a knock on his door, it startled him to the point of dropping the can. He cursed, but was happy it wasn't open yet. Who the hell was it? No one EVER came to his door. There were two times in the past five years when someone knocked on it, both times it was some suit wearing religious nut, but those knocks came in the afternoon, not nine at night. Suspicious, he edged to the door.

"Who's there?" Charlie yelled out. There was no answer, instead another knock, though this one sounded funny; it was followed by a scraping noise as if someone was dragging their knuckles down the door. Then the handle rattled. Looking back to the TV he saw a zombies head blow up. He thought about grabbing the shotgun he kept by the door but then the fair flashed in his mind, it was probably some drunk looking for a bathroom. Idiots. Relaxing, he grabbed the handle and swung the door open…the air in his lungs vanished when he saw, standing on the other side of the screen, right there on his own porch…a zombie.

It was Judge Fredrick, but a zombie version of him. His chubby face was even puffier than normal, his skin pale and worst of all? He had to have been eating brains. Red chunks and goo were all over his mouth and his white button down shirt. Charlie was frozen for a split second, the shock and beer incapacitating him, but when the judge's arms reached out for him, he moved. Moved so fast he tripped over his own feet backing up. The shot of pain that went from his tailbone down his legs when he hit the floor assured him he hadn't fallen asleep in his recliner, *this was real*. The Judge took a staggered, standard zombie like step towards him. Charlie was thankful he wasn't one of those fast movie zombies; he'd be dead if he was.

The Judge gurgled, stuttered a second and spit up some red goo, probably brains, it disgusted Charlie, but sent him into action. He could do this, he knew how to do this, all he had to do was get his shotgun and shoot the bastard in the head. Piece of cake. There was one shotgun by the door, but to get that he'd have to go past the zombie and he'd learned from the movies to never get within arm's reach. There was one in the barn, but that wouldn't help him, the one in the bedroom was the safest bet. Getting up he tripped on the beer can he dropped, fell onto his chest and cursed himself for drinking so much. As he gasped with pain, he felt a hand on his pant cuff, kicking frantically he got up and ran to the bedroom. Inside the room he held back tears as he grabbed the gun from under his bed and loaded it. The rest of the shells he stuffed into his pockets, if there was one zombie, there would be more.

With the gun ready Charlie told himself over and over again that he could do this, that he'd seen it done plenty of times, besides...*he was a man*. Aiming the gun at the bedroom door, he waited for the zombie Judge to try and break it down; he'd blast him as soon as he came in. His hands stung as sweat got into his cuts. Wiping his face he tried to calm his breathing, he'd never shot a human before. NO. It's not a human, Judge Fredrick is a zombie now, and zombies need to die. After not hearing any noise for a solid minute he decided he couldn't wait, if he did, his place might be swarming with those flesh eaters. With the barrel of the gun pointed at the door, he grabbed the handle and swung it open, the Judge wasn't there. With his legs quivering, Charlie walked down the hall towards the bathroom, the light was on. Zombies turn on lights? They didn't show everything in movies he guessed. A foot away from the door he took a deep breath, jumped into the pool of light and pulled the trigger.

The blast missed the Judge, he wasn't standing where Charlie thought he'd be, instead, he was leaning over with his face in the sink. Cocking the barrel, Charlie aimed again, told himself he never missed twice and pulled the trigger. The spray hit the Judge's head just as he was standing up. At first it looked like a giant puff of red, but as the echo of the blast faded, he could see the tiny splats of the hundreds of pieces of brain, skull and hair that hit the walls, ceiling and floor. In the movies, the zombies' brains were usually black and gunky, the Judge's was bright red; he must have just turned. Charlie stood staring at the mess and the crumpled body that fell half on top of the toilet. For some reason it didn't feel as cool as he thought blowing a zombie's head off would.

As the shock started to wear off he realized the front door was open, more of the bastards could get in. Rushing to the door he stopped in his tracks, he was too late, there on the steps, grasping onto the hand railing was Mary Lynn, the town beauty queen. She was wearing her tiara and soft blue, silky dress... that was covered in red slimy chunks. Though Charlie fantasized about her coming to his house many times, this was not what he wanted. This time, he didn't hesitate. As Mary Lynn's eyes got wide and her mouth fell open with a gurgle, he aimed and pulled the trigger. Her head exploded, sending her tiara up in the air, it landed on her body that was splayed over the stairs. This one made his stomach role, killing such a beautiful young girl made him...no, it was a zombie.

Looking out towards the field that was lightly lit with the fair's glow, he saw several more zombies making their way towards the house. There must have been an outbreak at the fair, if that was the case...the entire town was going to be affected. Looking around the porch he figured he had about three minutes before they reached him. Locking himself inside would make him a sitting duck, if they surrounded it, he'd die for sure. He had to get to his truck, take all the ammo he had and get out of Dodge. He could shoot as many as he could and make it out of town, maybe make it to the town over before it spreads, warn them, get a militia going. Man, the world was going to be so different.

Within ten seconds he had his keys in his hand and was running across the yard to the barn to get his truck. With the engine revved, he backed out, slamming into the door, sending it off the hinges. Peeling down the driveway Charlie suddenly hit the brakes, every less zombie is one less that can infect another person, maybe he could stop the spread before it got out of the town? Turning the wheel, the truck bounced off the road and spun its tires through the dirt of the freshly planted soybeans that Charlie worked so hard to get sprouting. There were four zombies in the field, they weren't that far apart, he could take them down. Pushing the gas all the way down the truck bumped and dipped violently. Seeing two zombies close together, he steered right at them. The first one slammed against his hood and disappeared under the wheels with a big bump; the other rolled over the windshield and landed with a thud in the bed of the truck. Charlie let out a howl of joy… *maybe this could be some fun.*

Jumping out of the cab he took three quick steps and fired at one of the last two zombies standing. The shot hit the young man in the chest, sending him to the ground. Cocking the gun he ran over, took aim and shot the head off. That left one more standing, the other two he still had to shoot their heads off to be safe, but they shouldn't be going anywhere with the damage the truck did to them. Reloading, he quickly walked to the other side of the truck. He was shocked to see the zombie was running away, they never ran away in the movies, they always just kept attacking…and this one was pretty darn fast. Not wanting to let the thing get away he jumped back in the truck and drove it back and forth a few times over the body until he saw the head pop off in his side mirror. The other one was still lifeless in the back of the truck, that one he could take his time with. By the time he started to chase down the last zombie it had almost reached the property line and the gate that lead into his neighbor's farm, where the fair was. Charlie only hoped that the rest of the people were not infected.

The zombie, who Charlie could tell by the jacket it was wearing, was one of the high school football kids, made it to the gate before he could run him down; it was going to be a foot chase. Charlie left the truck running and followed the zombie. The bright lights of the fairgrounds made his eyes ache for a second. As he squinted, he prepared himself to see all of the town folk slaughtered, when he saw that there were people walking around, without a care in the world, he couldn't understand what was going on. Looking around he finally caught a glimpse of the zombie rounding the corner of the Tea Cup ride. He had to get him before he got to anyone else; he had to save the town. Rounding the corner he suddenly slammed into a small crowd that gathered around the zombie.

"Get away! Get away, he is infected!" Charlie screamed swinging his gun in the crowd's face. People screamed and ran, though Doc Jones stayed with the zombie. The doc's arm was around the zombie teen, who also looked as if he had eaten brains…but if they had all eaten brains, where were all the bodies?

"Jesus Christ Charlie! What in God's name are you doing?" Charlie kept aim at the zombie, but looked around in case there were more. It was then he saw the stage and the giant sign that read *Cherry Pie Eating Contest Tonight!* Not seeing any more brain eaters he focused back at the two in front of him.

"Doc, he is a zombie, get away from him before he tries to eat your brains! Look at him for crying out loud, he's already eaten someone." The doc's face contorted, Charlie knew that if this was a movie, this would be the part that no one would believe him…until the zombie killed again.

"How stinking drunk are you Charlie? That is cherry pie on his face! The pie eating contest was tonight." Doc motioned to the sign behind him; Charlie started to feel a bit funny.

"Mabel screwed up. She dropped some cleaning chemicals in the pie mix but thought it wouldn't hurt anyone. It started to close up everyone's throats, they couldn't talk. The Montgomery's are having trouble with their plumbing so I sent them to your house to get water and because I gave you that case of EpiPens last month for your bee allergy. I figured you had about ten pens, you could shoot each one up and the epinephrine would clear their air passages. I was on my way over to help, but I had to attend to Mr. Carter, he thought he was having a heart attack... it was just gas though." Charlie's hand felt itchy, he wanted to pull the trigger, to kill the last zombie, but his mind suddenly started to hurt.

"Charlie, did you shoot them all up... please tell me you didn't. Hell, if you'd given them all shots, you'd be a hero for saving all of their lives.... Please tell me you gave them the shots." Charlie lowered the gun, looked over his shoulder at the dark field and the tiny orange glow of his living room light. The big climax would be playing in the movie now; zombies' heads would be popping all over the place.

"Yeah doc, I shot them all...."

# A GRAVE AFFAIR

For decades I lay in silence, biding my time, for what I do not know. Yet I lay and listened, listened as hard as I could, constantly. The first few years, they were magical. Everyone came. I would simply absorb everything they said, cherish it and play the words over in my mind during the silent hours. Then as time slipped by so quickly those silent hours became days, then weeks and months. Soon none of the words I heard were for me. They were simple conversations in the distance.

As the words slipped away, so did I. I changed, deteriorated, fell apart you might say. What was left of me I did not know, for I could not see anymore. I could only hear. It was the only trait I was left with. I couldn't move, though I tried many times only to achieve a flicker of movement, which I could never be sure if it was my doing or just a natural spurt of something. I was simply a set of ears, a set of ears that didn't exist.

I lived, though that is not the proper word, through what I heard. Sadly for decades I have heard practically nothing but sounds of nature and the occasional mechanical sounds of upkeep. Every once in a while I hear the crunching of footsteps, a cough, a sigh, a whistle and a few sneezes. But it's that rare gem, that diamond of sound I strain so hard to hear, that I long for, the human voice. At this point, it doesn't matter what they are saying. A simple word, any word, is enough to get me through days. It leaves a smile on my non-existent face.

Hearing words constantly, I understand it is hard for you to understand. But to hear nothing for years then to hear something as beautiful as "I love you", is like, well, the only joy I could compare it to is giving birth. And I should know, when I was alive I had seven children. The elation of hearing words after decades is almost the same as seeing something that has been growing inside of you for nine months. You'll understand some day.

A few years back I was lucky enough to have a school trip come through my section of the graveyard. At that point it was simply the best day I have ever had since I have been here. Hearing the laughter, the teasing the taunting of the sweet children's voices was like heaven. The scolding of the teachers made me laugh as it reminded me of my child raising years. The most magical, heart-breaking part was when a darling young boy read my headstone aloud: "Mary Elizabeth Crumb" Hearing my name I could feel the tears pour out of my nonexistent eyes. He kept reading. "Beloved Wife and Mother" He stumbled the words a bit and a teacher came over to help him read what I'm guessing is my fading letters. He continued "Aged 37 years. Wow, she died in 1878!" All this I knew of course, but then the teacher asked him, "Now how long ago was that?" My ears perked up, I had no clue. Time didn't have numbers in here, though at times I would try to count seconds and hours to kill time, countless times I tried to guess a year, but I knew I must have been wrong. And I was, by many, many years. "That means she died...over, one-hundred and twenty-seven years ago?" The teacher told the boy he was correct and if it was possible for me to faint, I would have. At most I thought I had been in the ground for only ten, maybe twenty years at most. It was a thought I contemplated for the next few years, until the next voices came, the ones that came again and again, the ones that changed my existence forever.

During those silent years after that, I mourned my children. I realized that all of them would be dead by now. Realizing this made me understand why no one has come to visit me in ages, why no one visited anyone in my section anymore. With a hundred years of deaths the cemetery must have become enormous. Leaving my section isolated in the past that is so far behind that even the generations below it are dead and gone. This was a hard realization for me. Yet there was nothing I could do about it. My depression would have sunk even deeper if it hadn't been for Clare and Robert.

It was a warm summer night when their loving voices first graced my ears. I only knew that fact because I heard Robert say so. Being in here I have no clue of the seasons, day or night. Because of this, I have always wondered why I am here. I was religious, prayed and fulfilled all my duties as a woman, mother, wife and child of God. Shouldn't I have gone to heaven? I doubted this was Hell, for besides the boredom and constant disorientation, it wasn't so bad. Purgatory was the only other option, but even then I could not understand why I would end up there.

Robert was the first voice I had heard. "You can't get much better than a beautiful summer night, with a beautiful girl." My pile of dust heart skipped a beat. A voice, an adult voice, so close to me. I perked up as much as I could, strained with all my might and listened for more. "I wouldn't exactly call being in a graveyard beautiful Rob. It's creepy." A woman as well! In a way I felt like I had a front row seat to an Opera, I was so excited.

"Clare, it might be creepy, but you'll get over it, because all that matters is us. We are alone, here together, finally, FINALLY."

"Are you sure no one comes around here?"

"Are you kidding me? This is the historic section, the only person that comes in here is the groundskeeper, once, twice a week tops to mow. It's night time, there are two trees here to block the view of us and besides we are so far back from the street no one could see us even if we stood waving a flag. We are safe here. Besides we talked about this, it's the last place in the world anyone would think to find us."

"I guess, it's, it's just a bit creepy."

"You'll get over it in time. Look, lay down the blanket here, it's nice and open. This will be our spot, our piece of the world that is ours and ours alone." Little did they know that piece of clear grass was right above me. I couldn't believe my luck. A couple was going to spend time with me. I held my breath and listened, hoping they would never leave.

They lay down, I could tell from the sounds, but at the same time, oddly enough, it was as if I could feel them through the ground, as if their love and warmth radiated down to me. They were silent for a few minutes and then I heard soft kissing. I melted with joy.

"This *is* nice. Maybe I can get used to it. And my god! Look at the stars above us." I could tell, or more so I hoped that he took her hand at this point and stared at the stars with her. It made me miss my husband Alfred, though he wasn't a romantic by any means, he still loved the stars.

"Is this crazy Clare? What we are doing? I mean…this is, well the truth is, I'm scared. I have never felt like this for anyone, not even my wife. I know we have only kissed so far, but tonight, tonight we can and might take it further. I'm afraid that if we do, I'll… I sound like such a wuss."

"No, no, go on please, please Rob."

"I just feel like if we get any closer, if I actually get to hold you in my arms and feel you against me, that I will fall in love with you, that my life will be changed forever." It stung me at first, to hear that he was married; I wanted them to be a young couple sneaking off to make love away from their parents prying eyes. I couldn't let my morals ruin this for me. Even if it was an affair, true love was what mattered. I waited to hear what the lady said in return.

"Rob, I'm already in love with you. I was before I ever talked to you. When I'm with my husband, when we are intimate, I shut my eyes tight and pretend it's you. I'm already past the point of return when it comes to you; I'll never be the same. I'm ready. And if my life has to change, if people have to be hurt so I can feel your love, then so be it." After that there were no words for a long time, just rustling on the ground. For a moment I felt guilty to be listening, I would have blushed if I could. Then I realized that this was better than any of those smut novels I secretly read when Alfred was out shipping, this was real, so I listened harder. I heard lips smack, clothing rustle and hands sliding over skin. They didn't make love though. No, they were going to save that, take their time and enjoy themselves, they were going to make it special. This made me more than excited, for when they were done pleasing each other with their hands, they vowed that this would be their spot from now on and that even down the road, years in the future, they would come back here every now and then. Hearing this made so joyous, for I had something to look forward to, finally.

That night they stayed long, longer than they should, so they said. I learned much about them and the world I have been withdrawn from for a century. The things they talked about, the devices and technologies were almost incomprehensible. Yet as they spoke of them and the times, I got a picture, a vague, blurry picture, in the back of my mind of the items they were talking about and I understood. As much as I needed to at least. Over the course of the past few months I believe I have grasped this modern age and devices that are so common. They are mind blowing to me, yet the fact that I can still think inside of this box after a hundred years is a little harder to grasp than the idea of being able to talk to someone through a device that you keep with you.

I learned the following information over the course of a long time; I will sum it up for you now, so you'll understand this couple. Robert had been married almost nine years and he had one boy aged five years. Clare had two little girls aged four and nine years, while she had been married eleven years. The part I liked the most was how they met. Robert was a jogger (something that was hard for me to understand at first) while Clare went out for a walk every night. The two would cross paths now and again, smile at each other and nod. Little did they know that they both were fantasizing about one another. Then one day, Clare pretended to trip while Robert was running by her. Like any chivalrous man he helped her up and the two began to talk. From then on out they stopped to talk to each other each time they passed, which became daily.

At first it was small talk and then it became long conversations. So long, that they skipped their walk and run to sit on the bench outside of the graveyard. Supposedly, they just knew they were going to have an affair. Neither of them made an advance at the other (which was the man's job in my day), they simply just started to talk about it as if it were inevitable. That's when the plans started. At first they tried to sneak away to one of their houses when no one was around, but that didn't work. It was too risky, especially with nosey neighbors. Then they planned on going to a motel, which I assume is like an inn. They were all set to go then realized they had to use a credit card (I'm still unclear what that is), that left evidence, which their spouses might find. With frustrations building, they decided to just enter the place they met in front of, at night. And that leads us to the first night I met them.

That first night for them, being intimate, holding each other loving, one another was a release of epic proportions. It was for me as well. It was as if I was released from my grave, I felt as if I was almost pulled closer to the surface by their love. When they left I replayed the conversation over and over. I tried to feel the love they had for each other. I tried to feel his hands on my, well my old body, the way they must have been on her. I spent hours, maybe even days, trying to picture what they looked like, what the clothing of this new century was. It was maddening not knowing. I wanted, needed, to know what they looked like.

The next time they showed up again, I was elated. At first they didn't even say words, a few giggles then it was an hour of almost straight kissing. It was brilliant. Hearing the heavy breathing, the gasps, smacks and moans of pure passion caused something amazing to happen, a miracle for me really. I felt something. Not emotionally, but physically. Something that hadn't happened since I was alive. It was subtle; you wouldn't have noticed it. Yet to me, it was like a horse rearing in fright. My finger, or more so the sliver of bone that is left of my right index finger, moved. Not much, not even enough that would warrant notice, but it moved and I felt it. It was so shocking that I lost track of the actions above me and waited to see if it would happen again. It did not that night.

The third night, they finally made love and it moved me, literally. The instant they both climaxed, what is left of my skeleton shuddered fast and hard for a full two seconds. Their love was giving me life. I felt myself cry that night. Not because I hoped I would come back to life, but because of their joy and being able to experience part of it.

They took off the next few nights and it scared me. I didn't know if they regretted going past the point of no return, but in my heart I knew they didn't. And thankfully they came back a few days later. The kisses were fast and hard that night. "I missed you, god I need you" flowed over their lips countless times. They had taken a few days off to make sure there was no suspicion. Thankfully they both thought there was none. That night they made love hard and fast, twice, within an hour. It was as long as they could be together to keep up the charade of going out for a walk and run. As they made love I tried to move my ancient limbs, it worked. Not much, but I was able to have control over my body, a flinch of the finger, a twinge of the hip. But only while they were one could I do this.

The time in between their visits I filled with waiting and trying to move. I thought of almost nothing else during these times, but of this couple. How I loved them as much as they loved each other. I wanted to move too, for one reason and one reason only: to see them. I *needed* to see them. Even though I could not see, I knew if I could make my way to the surface, I would be able to see them. *I just knew it.* Something told me it would be possible.

The next time they came I listened to their lovemaking and slowly, calmly tried to move. My arm

212

lifted up, I tried not to drop it from getting over excited. Then I moved my other arm. I was able to lift them both off the dirt and twist them a bit. The fingers were a bit rusty, but they too moved, one digit at a time. I then tried my neck, it moved as well, sending my head to the left and right ever so slowly. Each move filled with cracks and pops of protest. To my defeat the second they pulled away from each other, my arms fell back to my sides and my skull lolled to the left, frozen as it was for a hundred years.

Each time they came, I learned more about them, I loved them more and I loved my new found life with movement. Each time they made love I practiced moving every part of my body. A few pieces of me did not stay connected or work well, but I could move. I got it down to while they were making love I could feel around my prison, feel the roots that had grown through my casket over the years, the bugs that made a home in my chest cavity and the powdery substance of what was once my beautiful dress. After what felt like a month or so of their love giving me life, another miracle happened. I began to see. Just a split second at first. It was brilliant, the second they both climaxed, there was a giant flash and I could see everything inside of the coffin, even without any light. At first I was horrified to see my bones for the first time. But then the excitement that I could possibly see them, for real, overtook any horror at my own state.

The more they made love, the longer and more I could see. I took these flashes as chances to see how I could make my way to the surface to see them, to be with them, even if only for a second. My coffin had been made of fine wood at the time, but it had since deteriorated enough for a giant root to break through right above my chest. This hole allowed me to begin my work. While I had the ability to move, I slowly started to remove the pieces of wood above me, luckily the dirt held rather well. After a few sessions I was able to remove all of the wood leaving nothing but dirt and roots above me.

My next task was to start to dig my way upwards. It took a while to figure out how to do this, but I had a method and it worked well. I scraped at the ceiling with my boney fingers allowing the dirt to fall. The beauty of it was since I am only bone, the dirt falls right through me. All I have to do is dig, let it fall and adjust every now and then to position myself onto the fallen dirt. With each love making session I moved at least two inches toward the air above. It was wonderful. Time after time I made my way up closer and closer to them, feeling their love radiate through me. Then I heard words that filled me with dread. Winter was coming, they would have to find a new place soon, a place indoors.

Hearing this news made me move faster and faster at my digging, I had to see them before they left me forever. While they lay there in between their love making sessions, I listened to them hard. They talked about how it was time and that they could no longer hide out in a cemetery. They both loved each other more than they could say. They had to be with each other, they had to let the world know. Their spouses were getting suspicious as it was, a clean break was needed. They were to run away in three weeks. I could be mistaken, but I thought I felt a tear run down my cheekbone at the thought of losing them so soon. They then made love a second time and I dug with a furry like none other. When they finished I had my sight once again, this time for longer than a flash. A full five seconds went by. I looked at my stick finger, pushed it up above me and poked through the dirt, I had made it. I was only inches away from getting out, then they pulled apart, my movements ceased and my vision faded, but not before I got a glimpse of a star. It was the sweetest sight I have ever seen.

The next few days I was in agony. They did not show up. I was horrified they would never come back. I was so close, so close. If they made love one more time I could free myself, see them and be complete. If they never came back, I would be stuck where I was, so close to the earth. The rain would soak me, if someone walked over my area, they would sink in and crush my bones. I was scared.

Then, not too many days later, they showed up. This time I could sense that they had luggage of sorts with them. They ran into each other's arms and started kissing. To my amazement, I was able to move. I don't know why, but I believe it was their passion coming to fruition that gave me the ability. Slowly I moved my hands out to the surface. I was careful to go slowly to not distract them, to not make them panic. I needed to see them to be with them. The more earth I cleared, the quicker I realized I could see; it was brilliant. The stars greeted me first and then the glorious tree leaves above. I felt like I was finally ascending into heaven.

I was able to fully pull myself out of my grave and onto the grass without incident. Thankfully they had laid their blanket a bit further than normal. I took a second to look over my skeleton, amazed that I could move and see. Then I looked up to see my saviors for the first time. I cried. There they were, ten feet away rolling on the ground laughing, kissing. They were beautiful, everything about them. Their hair, eyes, skin, they were the perfect picture of passion and love. I wanted to get a closer look so I stood, it was hard at first, but I was able to get up and walk. The feeling, being able to see, feel air on my bones and to be free of my prison, I wanted to scream with joy,

215

but kept my jaw closed tight to not scare my heroes, besides I didn't know if words would come out.

Quietly as I could (for my bones rattled when I walked), I ducked behind the tree whose roots had made a home in my coffin. Rob was on his feet, his back against a tree himself. Clare was on her knees in front of him working at his pants. It felt wrong to be watching, but I couldn't look away, not until I heard a noise. It was subtle, something the couple didn't hear. It came from the other side of them. I leaned around my tree, looked at Rob's face in ecstasy and saw the other face off in the distance. There was a woman approaching as slowly as I was, going from tree to tree.

Instantly I knew it had to be his wife. She had found out and realized he was leaving her for good. I moved another tree closer, so close I almost felt high off of their pleasure. The woman was getting closer as well. I took a risk, skirted over to the very tree that my lovers were against and hid. It was then that I realized the reason for my resurrection.

It was the second snap of a stick that finally took Rob out of his own personal heaven. Clare herself kept going, thinking the groan of fear was pleasure until he grabbed her head and pulled her back away from him. It was immediately after the slurp of her mouth pulling away that I heard the sniffle of the woman behind them. I started to tremble, hoping my new found sight and energy wouldn't give out on me before my mission was done.

"So this is what the whore looks like?"

"Jesus Tiff! Where the hell did you get a gun?" I could hear Clare scramble to her feet as Rob zipped himself. Something told me to wait a few seconds more to intervene.

"It doesn't matter where I got it. It matters how I use it. At least after I kill both of you they won't have to

216

take you far to bury your sinning bodies! Hell, maybe I'll just bury the two of you myself. You guys planned on disappearing together anyways right? No one would ever find you then, you'd just be a dead beat missing dad, with an emphasis on dead."

"Do something Rob."

"Tiff, let me explain."

"There is nothing to explain, your dick was in her mouth, you have your luggage to leave me and the kids. End of story." I heard the cock of the gun and knew I had to move. My speed was amazing; within a second I was in front of my saviors. Everyone screamed, Tiffany shot the gun and it shattered one of my ribs, but thankfully did not go through to them. Tiffany looked at me with horror as I walked towards her. She shot four more times. Each shot miraculously hitting one of my bones, breaking them into tiny pieces. I let my jaw fall open, a hiss came out, then words. "GO, GO, GO!" I yelled over my shoulder. Tiffany remained still, trying to fire off more at me. When I reached her she started to laugh, thinking what was happening was not real. But it was.

My strength was another amazing feat. In death I was stronger than I ever was in life. With my right hand (the other arm I could not move since the bones had been shattered) I grabbed the scorned wife and dragged her back to my grave. At first I did not know what I was doing but then I realized I knew what to do all along. I wrapped my boney hand around her throat and squeezed. She dropped the gun, looked at me, gasped for breath, irked out the word *please* and turned purple. For a second I was appalled by what I was doing, killing an innocent woman who was only guilty of being hurt, then I realized, my freedom was in her death. I squeezed harder.

Then it began. My rebirth and her death. As her blood vessels closed off and she began to die, chunks of her flesh started to fall from her face and arms. Her eyes started to shrivel up. As for me, muscle, veins and tendons rapidly grew over my body. Just a thin layer at first, then more and more appeared as she died. Tiffany became the skeleton I was and I became the woman she was. When the transformation was complete I held nothing but a spine in my newly flesh covered hands. I let the bones drop on the soft earth I had come out of only minutes before. As if it were quick sand they sunk in and disappeared within seconds, leaving me to look over my naked body. I was human again, I was whole.

Lightning bolts of pain shot through my skull, I fell to my knees, clasped my head and watched the images of Tiffany's life pass through my mind's eye. I had acquired all of her memories, her thoughts, everything about her. It was then that I realized I had become her; I was not the woman I was before I died. I was Tiffany, at least physically. I started to cry not knowing if having life again was a curse or a blessing. I was free to live, but because someone else died.

After crying for several minutes I heard footsteps behind me. It was my lovers. They were approaching with caution. They had seen the whole transformation. Without saying anything Rob swooped in and grabbed the gun from the ground.

"What have you done with my wife? What did you do?" I stood up slowly, raised my arms out in plea.

"I saved your lives. And mine. I only did what I had to do." A few minutes later I was clothed in one of Clare's outfits she had packed. When the sun came up, I felt its glorious rays of heat hit my face, my new face, I cried again. I did that a lot over the next few months…as I *lived*.

# IN THE END... DEATH WINS

There is nothing more peaceful than embalming a body. With some light classical music playing in the background, the slow flow of the blood flowing through the tube and the silence of a dead body, one can truly relax. Unlike in the outside world, the one aboveground, with windows and loud noises and people who complain, the room of an embalmer is magical. It is their own space in the world, their silent wonderful sanctuary. Just them and a body or two.

During the bed bug epidemic, Jonathan thought this wonderful world would come crashing down around him. They were burning the bodies in mass graves. There was no need for a mortician. Those few months were the worst in his life. He almost went broke and worst, his sanity almost cracked as he had no bodies to make beautiful. Then the cure came, bodies no longer had to be burned, people suddenly wanted to bury their loved ones again. Business boomed, more than any time in history. Almost fifty funerals a week and that was only because that was all Jonathan could handle. If he could have done more, he would have.

One particular woman during that time, Jane something, was in horrible shape; bald, cut up and the back of her own head was blown off. It was the biggest challenge Jonathan ever faced. It took him almost two days to make the woman acceptable for viewing. His work was so miraculous that they were able to have an

219

open casket. It was one of his proudest moments. When the cure kicked in, the flow of bodies returned to normal, but there was an odd influx in strange deaths and occurrences that intrigued Jonathan though he loved it, something felt wrong about it all.

Right after the bug epidemic, one particular funeral had Jonathan on edge. A man's wife and daughter had died. The man was irate, throwing fits and yelling at everyone. It was over the top, and more than suspicious. Jonathan pinned the guy for killing his family, but he didn't report it, bodies were business after all. And hell, he liked the guy, he had balls, so he ignored it. The very next day, two bodies came in that were stitched, glued and stapled together. It was a fascinating mess that Jonathan relished every minute of. Cutting them apart, fixing the holes and tears was like putting together an amazing puzzle. Not even a few days later at the funeral home's sister mortuary, one of its workers, Ani, was found dead, having pumped herself full of embalming fluid after stealing a body. *What the fuck was going on?* Jonathan started asking himself at this point. With this much shit going on it had to be the end of the world.

That very week, three bodies showed up in the very graveyard he sent most of his bodies too. This made Jonathan's skin itch, having taken the "bed bug cure", he knew it wasn't them, it was merely the creeps settling in. With this many bodies showing up, something bad was going to happen. When he met a strange, yet beautiful woman at his bar that was a bit... too friendly, he turned her down. Two days later he found out about the "God's Whores" cult. He couldn't believe how lucky he was, but again, that feeling kept creeping in, something very bad was coming. He knew that for a fact when numerous bodies showed up after the county fair with no heads.

When a body sucked of its fat showed up and the crunched up body of a man who jumped out of a window with his dead girlfriend's body parts in his hands, he knew it was time to prepare. Halloween was only a few days away, meaning more shit would probably happen. He loved the business, but the deaths were getting too close to him. After a few days of shopping, Jonathan was stocked with weapons and enough rations to get him through the end of the world, which might just have been coming. Halloween was amazingly uneventful, though the day after he received a body of a teen that was stabbed to death and used as a prop in a haunted house. *One more, just one more body comes in... and I'm gone.* Jonathan told himself. In his thirty years stuffing bodies he had maybe, maybe five odd deaths or murders and in the last month he had dozens. Something was going to happen.

When the coroner brought in a few, decaying, hacked apart bodies with holes cut in it where some sicko had sex with the corpses, Jonathan didn't even bother embalming the bodies. He merely took one look, went upstairs, grabbed his bags and went out to his travel camper and drove off. It was a fifteen minute drive to get out of the populated part of town and another twenty to get out of the town limits. He only hoped he could make it that far. As the sweat started to pour down his face, he thought of all the bodies he saw, the odd and weird ways they died. He remembered the news article he read that morning about a man who killed his neighbor for pissing on him, he knew that body would be coming to him as well, if he hadn't left. Death after death flashed before his eyes, the dead were haunting him, *death*, was coming for him.

As he passed by his sister and brother-in-law's house, he thought about the man they said to have seen at the end of their bed. Was that death watching his family?

Waiting for the right moment to claim them too? With a few deep breaths he tried to relax, twenty more minutes and he'd make it out of town... and be safe. Passing the graveyard he knew too well, he thought about his father and the stories he told him about how he too once almost had death catch up to him. It was after burying the bodies from not one, but two serial killers, one that used his mother's head as a dart board and another who cut the intestines out of his victims that his father said he only lived because... because, Jonathan was born. He said that just as death was about to kill him, he saw a *life*, and was scared off. He never believed the story, just like he never believed his girlfriend who told him she had risen from the grave after being dead for decades, but now, maybe he had to believe these stories.

Ten minutes from the county line he screeched to a halt. Maybe the town line wasn't the answer, it was life, new life. That was how to scare off death. He needed to show death a newborn, it worked for his father, why not for him? Five minutes and a few quick turns later, he found himself taking up half a dozen parking spots at the local hospital. Racing into the building, looking over his shoulder the entire time, he ran up to the directory, scrolled his finger down the list and found the maternity ward was on floor four. Scratching his arms furiously, he got on the elevator and pushed the button for the fourth floor twenty times.

As the doors opened and he walked out, he stopped in his tracks at an odd picture hanging on the wall. Feeling the pressure to move on, but curious nonetheless, he stopped and looked. It was of a bearded woman and several "freaks", they were smiling and handing over a check to a doctor. The inscription read: *Maternity Ward Donation Given By the Side Show of The Zambean Circus, 1923"*. He couldn't figure out why the picture fascinated him, he wanted to look at it for hours, but time was short, he had to force himself away and find a baby.

Feeling dizzy halfway down the hall, Jonathan ran into the bathroom to splash water on his face, he had to have a clear head. Looking up he saw his reflection, he looked horrible, as if death was already setting in. Then his eye caught the reflection of another mirror and he panicked. The memory of an old wife's tale about staring into infinity by putting two mirrors in front of each other could cause you to die or disappear. With one swift punch, he shattered the mirror and the left the room. His hand ached, it dripped bright drops of blood down the hall and every time he moved his fingers he could feel the glass grinding under his skin, but he moved on… he had to.

People stared at his hand and at him. Nurses asked if he was ok but he ignored them all has he rushed to the nursery. There was a code broadcast over the overhead speakers, but he ignored it. Death was on his shoulders and he could feel it. *Just a few more feet… and everything will be alright.* Jonathan promised himself. When he saw the glass wall and the dozens of babies behind it, he started to laugh hysterically, he made it, he really made it. With a quick look behind the glass, he was satisfied they were all newborns, maybe only hours old, this much "new life" would definitely scare off death. Grabbing the door handle, it didn't move, why didn't he realize it would be locked? Across from the window was a row of chairs, three of which were empty, the other five full of exhausted looking parents and grandparents. Ignoring them, he grabbed a chair and used every drop of energy he had to smash it into the window. Being only one pane thick and old, it shattered instantly. Seeing the shards fly over the babies made his heart drop a bit but he didn't have time to worry about a few nicks. He had to get one and show it to Death as he could feel the icy hands on his back now. Trying to shrug them off as he put his leg on the ledge to jump into the room, he realized it wasn't Death, it was one of the dad's attempting to stop him. Grabbing the small handgun off his belt, the one that had been there since he stocked up on weapons, was an instant reaction. The second the dad saw the gun, the man backed off. Jonathan sighed, it was just a matter of hopping in and grabbing one now.

Pointing the gun at the father, he told him to back up and then carefully tried to put one leg over the window frame. As his leg rested on the jagged glass edge, he felt death enter his body, he was too late. Looking down at his chest he saw the bullet hole. *So that is the form death was taking today,* Jonathan thought as he fell to the ground, his one leg dangling in the air as his pant leg was stuck on a shard of glass. As he watched the blood leave his body, light danced in front of his eyes and noise from the outside world vanished. A bullet wound was easy to fix, as long as it wasn't on the face. Jonathan had seen many of them in his day. He'd love to fix up a body with a big chest wound, instead, someone else would be doing his job, for once, *he'd* be the body on the table. It was only fitting he guessed.

While his breath slowed, he laughed inside his own head, death was a funny bastard, he could get you in so many ways.

# ACKNOWLEDGMENTS

I'm not one for thank yous or speaking to the living, but I must give some gratitude to some people, for without them, this book would never have come out.

First and foremost, I'd like to thank Michael Aloisi for pushing me to take my dark secrets and horrible thoughts out of coffins and let them free in the world. While I was and still am hesitant to let people read my work, there is something deeply gratifying in getting these out there. Thank you Michael.

While I will not name the funeral home I work for, I would like to give them a huge thanks for the years of work they have given me. Letting me live in the home with the dead I love so much and graciously allowing me to spend hours on making bodies beautiful has been the kindest act anyone has ever done for me. Without the dead, I would be lost, thank you for not letting me lose myself.

Missy Gordon, thank you for reading the first manuscript. I was hesitant when Michael asked me to let you read the book, but your insight, kindness, thoughts, suggestions and help took this book from being a bunch of stories to a magical experience of the macabre. Thank you for being as sick as me…I will forever be indebted to you. If you ever go before me, I hope I have the opportunity to prepare you for the greatest journey of rest.

A special thank you to artist Joel Robinson for creating an amazing cover for my book. Make sure to visit his website at www.ArtPusher.net.

To Mr. B, Ms. E and Ms. R, preparing your bodies for rest had a magical experience on me. I cannot explain why or how you had so much impact on me, but spending time with your silent corpses inspired me to write and write… may you rest in peace.

# ABOUT THE AUTHOR

Michael Gore was born in a small town in New England. His earliest memory is of his father standing above him with a bloody knife. Being that his father was a butcher, he was around blood and raw meat his entire childhood. It is probably why at a young age he was fascinated with dead animals and even ended up in therapy at the age of nine for "finding out what made them tick." After that he learned to keep his curiosity to himself.

At sixteen he was a horror film fanatic. Not only did he watch every slasher film he could get his hands on, he took it a step farther and got a job at a local funeral home even though he already worked sixteen hours a week cleaning intestines for his father to make sausage out of. After several years of cleaning up the funeral home they let him assist in the embalming practice. This only fed into his appetite for the macabre.

Though his father wanted him to take over the butcher shop, Michael decided to play with human flesh instead of animals. In 2000 he graduated from mortuary school and secured employment as a mortician. During school, he started to write stories in his dorm room to avoid having to talk to his roommate and other classmates. Along with being a mortician, writing became his second passion.

Now, in-between draining bodies of blood, Michael spends his time writing, though he will only write while he is in the embalming room. When asked why he writes such dark things he only replied with, "to keep me from doing them in real life."